MW01136808

Electing to Love

Kianna Alexander

For Kay
Thanks for your
support !
Kianna Alexander

Kianna Alexander

Kianna Alexander

Electing to Love
Roses of Ridgeway, Book 4

© Copyright 2015
by E. M. Manning
writing as Kianna Alexander

Kianna Alexander

Kianna Alexander

*-In Loving Memory o f McNeil Pettiford
We'll never forget you, Papa Mac-*

Kianna Alexander

Kianna Alexander

Electing to Love

Kianna Alexander

Chapter 1

Angel May Lane hoisted the hand painted wooden sign above her head again, her feet keeping pace with the marching of her friends. Raising her voice, she chanted along with them.

"We demand the vote! We demand the vote!"

She and six of her female friends were circling on foot in the center of town, at the intersection of Ridgeway's only two major roads- Town Road and Founder's Avenue. Their small town, about fifteen miles northeast of Oakland, was home to a population of just under two thousand people. The town itself encompassed about twenty square miles, and every passing year seemed to bring new growth and change. Ridgeway now had a library, a general store, barber and beauty shops, and a travel depot where stagecoaches arrived and departed to connect folks to the train routes in Oakland. The jewel of town, the three story Taylor Hotel, sat behind them on the northeast corner of the two roads. No other small town in the area could boast such well appointed accommodations. And with her saloon, the Crazy Eights, plus Lilly's Dress Emporium, Ruby's Eatery, and Hats by Zelda, there were four female owned businesses in town.

If women here were capable enough to run profitable businesses, then why couldn't they vote? Why shouldn't they? It was a question she'd grown tired of asking, so she and some of the others had decided to act. They weren't little girls acting out to get their way, no matter how much the men tried to characterize them that way. Angel was thirty three years old, a full grown adult, and she was one of the younger members of the group.

She looked up and down the road at the folks around her, beyond the women who'd come to fight for the cause of suffrage. There were mothers walking their children to the schoolhouse, business people opening their various shops, and men driving through town on the way to begin a hard day's work. Some were wealthy, some were poor. There were whites; there were people of color, and some of mixed heritage. While some of them didn't agree with what she and her friends were doing, she didn't see them as enemies. No, when she looked around at the faces of these people, she saw her neighbors.

She looked upon them all in kindness, but that would not hinder her cause. Women deserved the right to vote, and she and her friends aimed to bring attention to the issue, in the hopes of bringing about a positive change. Their presence drew a lot of attention from the townsfolk carrying out their business in town, and effectively shut down most vehicle traffic.

"Go home where you belong!' shouted one angry man seated atop a listing old buggy that had seen better days.

Others trying to traverse the intersection shared his view, and made their opinions known.

"Yeah, take your nonsense elsewhere!"

"Get out of the road!"

All around her, the shouted protests of angry drivers rang out, at times drowning out the chant Angel and her friends continued to repeat in loud, boisterous tones.

One man, having given up on getting anywhere in his buckboard, threw his hands up. She watched as he set his hand brake, climbed down from his vehicle on the eastern side of the intersection, and struck out on foot. Apparently he'd gotten frustrated enough that he didn't mind leaving his carriage in the middle of the road. As he passed by her, he glared.

"I don't have time for such foolishness, I have an appointment!" He muttered the words through a clenched jaw as he made his way up Founder's Avenue, leaving his vehicle and horse parked in the middle of the road.

While she didn't relish inconveniencing her neighbors, she did believe her cause was a worthy one. In less than a month's time, the men of Ridgeway would report to the polls and cast their vote for a new mayor as well as the next President of the United States. Due to Bernard Ridgeway's decision to retire, the seat would be open, and two candidates were out rustling up votes. While she knew who she favored in both races, she also knew it didn't much matter what she, or any other female citizen of town thought, unless they could cast a ballot.

The women of Ridgeway didn't consider their demand unreasonable; after all, they were not asking for the right to vote in the upcoming presidential race. All they wanted was a say in the political landscape of their own town. Angel and the other women all agreed that local suffrage should come first. If that could be achieved, then they'd go on with their work to win state voting rights, and beyond. It was their fervent hope that someday, any woman in the country would have the right to vote in any and all elections. But in order to reach that goal, the work had to begin somewhere. Angel and the other women thought it may as well be here, on the streets of their tiny little California town.

So, in the midst of the angry shouts, threats, and curses being hurled at her by the drivers trying to navigate the road, they marched on, holding their signs high and echoing the chant.

As Angel passed the entrance to the Taylor Hotel for what seemed like the ninetieth time, a tall, broad figure stepped into her path.

She walked right into him, colliding with him so that her nose was crushed against the hard plane of his chest, level with his shoulders.

Her sign fell out of her hand, and landed on the hard packed dirt road with a thud.

Behind her, the bank clerk Daisy Trice walked smack into her back.

Raising her head, Angel looked into the dark, storm-filled eyes of Deputy Gregory Simmons. The burnished face held a proud nose, full lips, and bore the shadowy remnants of a missed opportunity to shave. He was as painfully handsome as always, but his expression conveyed disdain, perhaps even anger.

"Deputy..." she stammered as more of her compatriots crashed into each other like the wayward cars of a derailed train. Gathering her composure as best she could, she plastered on a smile. "Have you come to join our cause?"

One of his thick eyebrows lifted. "You know I haven't. I told you that if you and your ladies held up traffic again, I would arrest you."

She cocked her head, remembering the threat he'd uttered just three days ago, when she and her cohorts had staged a similar protest in front of the recently opened Ridgeway Travel Depot. "I remember you saying that. But I didn't think you'd actually do it."

A smile holding very little humor lifted the corners of his mouth as he removed a pair of handcuffs from his belt. "Ah, but I was quite serious, Ms. Lane." Deftly, he grasped one of her hands and snapped the cuff onto it, then reached for the other.

She could feel her jaw tightening with indignation. How could he do such a thing? "You're actually going to arrest me? Surely you see the logic in letting women have the vote, don't you, Deputy?"

He shook his head as he fastened her other hand into the cuffs. "Yes, I am arresting you- Sheriff Rogers' orders. And no, I don't see the logic in letting women vote."

She narrowed her eyes. "Why not? We've got just as much right as..."

He rolled his eyes, raising a dismissive hand. "Spare me. The fact that you're out here disturbing the peace and blocking traffic shows just how irrational and foolish you women can be. Now tell your friends to disperse, or they'll all be cooling their heels in the cell right along with you."

She could feel her face fold into a deep scowl. "Why, I

never!"

"First time for everything, Miss Lane." He grasped the steel chain linking the cuffs with one hand, and placed the other hand on her waist. With a firm but gentle motion, he turned her around to face the other ladies.

She trembled at the contact of his hand so near her denim clad hip. The heat from his fingertips penetrated the layers of cloth, making her feel as if they were touching, skin to skin. She had the strangest sensation of wanting the touch to last, of wanting more sensual contact with him.

His gruff words cut through her fantasy. "Miss Lane, send your friends away. Now."

Snatched back to reality, she drew a deep breath. Looking at Daisy, Prissy, and the others who had gathered to protest, she shook her head. She felt a very real sense of defeat. When she'd left the Crazy Eights this morning toting her sign, she'd never imagined she'd be arrested like a common criminal.

Daisy, her eyes wide, spoke. "Lord, Angel. Is he really going to haul you in?"

She nodded. "Ladies, you all best be getting home. There's no sense in all of us going to jail."

Lupe, who tended bar at the saloon, stepped forward. "Don't worry, Angel. We'll have you bailed out before nightfall."

The others all expressed their agreement, and that brought a smile to her face. Knowing she could depend on her friends made accepting this travesty of justice a bit easier. Turning back toward Deputy Simmons with pursed lips, she gave a single nod. "Let's go, Deputy."

"We will, as soon as I see these ladies disperse." His dark eyes scanned the assemblage of women.

Lupe tucked a dark ringlet of hair beneath her flowered hat. "Come on, ladies." She started walking away from the intersection, staying to the plank walk and headed in the direction of the saloon. The other ladies followed suit.

Kianna Alexander

As if satisfied, Gregory began walking Angel up Founder's Avenue toward the structure housing the sheriff's office and jail.

Once inside, he undid the cuffs and escorted her into the first of three empty cells. When he closed the iron bars and locked her in, she sat down on the short wooden bench situated against the rear wall of the cell.

Her handsome, but surly captor walked away, leaving her to contemplate her current situation. Her eyes darted around the room, taking in the sights. The bench she sat on, and the low cot in the corner, were the only furniture in the space. Above her head, there was a single, square shaped window hewn out of the stone wall. Though it was not very large, the window was still outfitted with three short iron bars.

She couldn't help wondering if the murderous Crazy Charlie had been incarcerated in this cell. Three years prior, the outlaw had killed Doris Ridgeway, a prominent citizen of town. It outraged her to think that she, an upstanding, taxpaying citizen of town, would be thrown into a cell with only slightly more regard than a hardened criminal like him.

Now that she was in the quiet of the cell, away from the commotion outside, she remembered something the deputy had said. Recalling his accusations made her even madder, and she resolved that if she were going to be stuck here all day, she would make the best use of it by giving him a good sized piece of her mind.

To that end, she stood and came to the door of the cell. A glance to her right let her see him, sitting at the desk at the end of the hall, just a few feet away. The dark waves of his brown hair barely grazed the base of his neck. He appeared to be writing something, and was a bit hunched over the desktop.

In any other situation, she might have hesitated to interrupt whatever he was doing. But right now, she didn't care what he was busy with.

He was going to hear her, and hear her good.

She opened her mouth and shouted, "Deputy! I need a word with you!"

***

Gregory looked up from his arrest report when he heard Angel shrieking for him. A groan escaped his lips. Whatever she wanted would likely be a waste of his time, but responding to her request was the professional thing to do. With that in mind, he lay down his pen, got up, and took the few steps down the corridor to the first cell.

She stood there, her small hands propped on her denim clad hips. If her tone hadn't given away her displeasure, her posture and facial expression made it clear. Her full lips were pursed so tight they almost disappeared, and he noticed the same tightness in the chocolate brown jaw. Angel's hazel eyes were flashing with fire and brimstone, and he braced himself for a lecture of some sort. "Yes, Ms. Lane?"

"You called me irrational. I demand an apology!"

He wanted to chuckle, but held back, thinking the better of it. "I didn't call you irrational. I called all women irrational. The fact that you 'demand' anything, when I'm the law and you're the prisoner, proves my point."

She gripped the bars, and narrowed her eyes. "How dare you say such things? Do you presume to know every woman in the world, to make such blanket judgments about an entire sex?"

He shrugged. "I don't need to know all of you. The few I've met have all proven to be crazy on some level."

A sound of utter disgust erupted from her mouth. "How much will it cost my friends for you to release me from this den of charlatans?"

Kianna Alexander

"Seventy-five dollars, the fine for disturbing the peace. If you ladies stop parading around making silly demands, I won't have to arrest you again."

She folded her arms across her chest, squaring her shoulders. "Silly demands, you say? Tell me, Deputy, what do you know about politics?"

He grazed his fingertips over his chin. Venom spitting aside, Angel Lane was a beautiful woman. Chocolate skin, a mop of wavy dark hair that reached her shoulders, and as shapely a figure as he'd ever seen on a woman. With her penchant for tight denim trousers and frilly collared blouses, like the ones she wore now, he could easily make out the curves beneath.

"Deputy, I'm waiting."

Her impatient tone wasn't lost on him and it was enough to draw his attention back to the present, and the question she'd asked him. "I know that Noah is running against Nathan Greer for mayor, since Bernard's decided to retire."

"And? Don't you know anything further?"

"I know who I'm going to vote for, what more is there to know?"

She shook her head, as if she pitied him. "What do these men stand for? And what of the national elections? America will choose a president this year as well, if you didn't know."

She might think him dim-witted, but he when knew he was being insulted. "I know there's a presidential election going on, I'm not an idiot. I just don't care much for politics."

"Hmph." She gave him a rather dismissive look.

He could see from the tight set of her face that she meant to rile him, but he remained calm. Folding his arms across his chest, he leaned his back against the wall opposite the cell. "I already know who I favor in the mayor's race here, what more do I need to know?"

She blew out a breath, her hazel eyes rolling as if she were speaking to a child. "Do you really think the mayor's race in a little town like Ridgeway is the only important vote you need to make? What about the presidential race?"

He shrugged. He'd never had much interest in national politics. "I'm not of a mind that my vote counts much when it comes to that."

"Come now. You're a white man, and voting is your birthright. Do you really take it for granted so much that you don't even bother to inform yourself about national elections?"

He didn't like her tone, but fought to keep his expression neutral. "I suppose so. And I suppose you're going to teach me the err of my ways."

She harrumphed, flopped down on the bench inside the cell. "Not sure I can do that. But I can tell you all about the facts in the presidential race."

He watched as she leaned back against the cell's wall, and slung one long, lean leg over the other. The demure positioning somehow managed to cause a tightening in his groin. Clearing his throat as he dragged his gaze upward to her face, he nodded. "Go ahead. My shift's not over till this afternoon."

Raking a graceful hand through her dark locks, she started in. "As you know, Grover Cleveland in the Democrat incumbent in the race-- you do know he's the current president, correct?"

He cut her a hard look, but nodded.

Her face softened a bit, and she continued. "Senator Benjamin Harrison, of Indiana, is the Republican candidate running against him, along with his vice presidential candidate, a mister Levi P. Morton."

He looked at her between the iron bars, amazed by the way her hazel eyes danced with light as she listed the facts of the election. It was a topic most folks, including him, found endlessly dull. Somehow, Angel May managed to be enthralled with it.

"There are a few other candidates- Clinton B. Fisk of the

Prohibition Party, Alson Streeter of the Union Labor Party, and of course Belva Lockwood, the only female candidate-she represents the National Equal Rights Party. Out here, though, she'll likely be a write in."

That last sentence gave him pause. "So there's a woman in the race? Running for President of the United States?"

She pursed her full, pink tinted lips. "Sure there is, and why not? She's run before, back in '84." She paused, touched a fingertip to her chin. "I can see why you're surprised, though, seeing as how you think women too stupid to vote, let alone run for office."

He felt a tinge of guilt, but vowed not to reveal it to her. She was already high and mighty enough without him playing into her little tirade. Grasping the bridge of his nose between his thumb and forefinger, he groaned. "Yeah, sure. Just go on and tell me, then. I suppose you'd vote for Lockwood, then, if you could vote?"

She shook her head, her expression giving away her distaste. "Tisk, tisk, Deputy. Once again you think you know all there is to know about women, and once again, you're wrong. I don't base my political decisions on gender."

He felt his jaw tighten as a bit more of his patience with this smart mouthed, headstrong woman slipped away. "Cut the sass and tell me who you'd vote for, Ms. Lane."

She tapped her chin again before she spoke. "Actually, I favor the Prohibition party candidate, Fisk. He was a Union general in the War Between the States, a senior officer of the Freedman's Bureau, and has done a lot of good work for education in the south."

Once again, she'd surprised him with her knowledge of the world. He was still not of a mind that all women were so well informed, though. His own mother had never even mentioned anything remotely political, and really had seemed content with her sewing, washing and cooking.

"Enough about my view. As a man, you ought to know what's going on, since you've got the vote. The main issue of this election is tariff policy--"

He cut her off. "That much, I know. Noah and I read an AP article about it in the Sacramento paper. Cleveland favors lower tariffs and Harrison favors them higher. Aside from that, Cleveland is against pensions for veterans of the war, and Noah and I don't cotton to that."

Her eyes widened, and a faint smile lifted the corners of her full lips.

"See? I'm not such a dullard on these topics as you thought." He felt the satisfied smirk creep over his face, and did nothing to hold it back.

Her smile broadened in response. "Aren't you something? There may yet be hope for the male race."

Seeing her beautiful smile and hearing the humor in her voice made him chuckle. "I guess I can say the same for the female race."

A peal of laughter erupted from her mouth.

Perched on the bench, laughing as if she hadn't a care in the world, she was as beautiful a creature as he'd ever seen. She threw her head back, the dark waves of hair falling away to reveal the lovely contours of her chocolate-skinned face. Her pert bosom, the round tops revealed by the flouncy lace collar of her blouse, bounced in time with her giggles.

He was enraptured. The lovely, mirthful lady before him bore precious little resemblance to the angry faced snapping turtle he'd arrested earlier. Now that he'd had time to survey her, from the crown of her dark hair to the flat soled brown leather boots on her small feet, he couldn't ignore her lush, dark beauty. He'd never spent this much time regarding a woman of color, and this one seemed to posses a certain quality that made him wonder why.

She managed to tamp down her laughter, and drew a deep breath. "What time is it?"

He pulled the pocket watch out of the inner pocket of his buckskin vest and glanced at it. "Half past noon. Got somewhere to be?"

She shook her head. "No, and I'm sure Lupe can handle things at the saloon until I'm bailed out. I know my aunt Myrna will be upset about all this, though, and I'd like to see to her as soon as possible."

"Ah, I see." He was quite familiar with her aunt, who often played piano at the Crazy Eights. Myrna was over the age of sixty, and a retired stage actress. From everything he'd seen, Angel loved her aunt very much, and made caring for her a high priority.

She leaned forward, propping her elbow on her knees and resting her chin in her upturned palms. Her eyes mirrored the concern in her voice. "I hope she remembers to take her medicine. If she gets wrapped up in a book, she'd forget all about it, and next thing you know I'll be taking her down to Doc Wilkins' clinic."

He remembered Lupe's promise to bring bail money to the jail later in the day. Nothing in his interactions with her made him think her dishonest, so he made a decision. Removing the ring of keys from the waistband of his denims, he searched through them for the key to Cell #1. "Tell you what, I'll prove I'm reasonable by letting you go a bit early, so you can see to your aunt's care."

She perked up, scooting to the edge of the bench. "Truly? You would do that?"

He nodded, locating the correct key. Inserting it into the lock, he turned it. "Yes, but there are conditions. You must pay your fine no later than five o'clock this evening, and you must give me your solemn vow not to let your protests interfere with traffic again. Agreed?"

Already on her feet, she waited near the door. "Yes, yes, I promise. Will you get into trouble with Noah for this?"

"Long as the fine is paid by day's end, all's well." He opened the door, and as it swung open into the hallway, she stepped out into the narrow corridor.

The door swung shut behind her, and she took a single

step backward.

The movement, along with the tight space of the hallway, caused the back of her body to make contact with the front of his. Her back grazed his chest, and her comely, round bottom pressed against the front of his denims.

His body reacted to her closeness, and the sweet floral scent floating up from the bare column of her throat. Heat filled him, and it seemed every bit of blood running through his upper body took a southward turn. His hands, of their own accord, came up to rest on her hips. His palms burned, his mind wandering to all the scandalous things he could have demanded in exchange for her release. But he was not that kind of man.

The contact lasted several long moments before she gasped. Her body tensed against his, her back becoming stiff; rigid.

Heart pounding in his ears, he dragged his hands away, knowing such boldness wasn't proper between a man of the law and an unmarried woman of town.

She sidled away, putting a bit of distance between them. When she looked up at him, her face cheeks glowed a rosy flush of heat. "Why, Deputy. If I didn't know better, I'd say you were being a little bit fresh."

He stammered a bit as he searched for the right words. "I...forgive me....my apologies, Miss Lane. That wasn't appropriate."

She blinked a few times. "It's quite alright. Thank you for allowing me to leave, Deputy."

He gave a solemn nod. "Sure. Just remember your promise."

She showed him her back as she walked up the corridor, into the front office and toward the door. As she stepped to the threshold, the afternoon sun casting a brilliant glow on her dark halo of wavy hair, she paused. "Good day, Deputy."

"Good day Miss Lane. Please, call me Gregory. And again, my apologies for my behavior."

The golden, feline eyes locked with his. "Apology accepted, Gregory. And just so you'll know, it wasn't altogether unpleasant."

His mouth fell open.

A ghost of a smile crossed her face, then she turned and walked out, soon disappearing into the gaggle of townsfolk moving up and down the plank walk.

Shaking his head in the wake of her brazen words, he sat on the edge of the desk and looked out the door for a long while.

Chapter 2

Gregory sat back in the wooden chair he occupied, taking a sip from a tin mug of coffee. Today was his first day off in nearly two weeks. Instead of sleeping in, he'd risen early to make his way here to Buck's Barbershop. He ran a hand over his shaggy hair as he waited for the chair to open up, and lamented again at how overdue he was for a shave and haircut.

Edward "Buck" Buckner, the town's barber, snipped the ends of hair hanging in the face of his patron, a man Gregory didn't recognize. "Be done in just a minute, Greg."

He offered a nod, then cast his eyes toward the door. Propped open by a large stone, the doorway acted as a portal for him to view the goings-on outside the shop. The day had dawned misty and foggy, and remained that way now that the breakfast hour had passed. The citizens of Ridgeway went about their business as usual, undaunted by the cloud shrouded, gloomy conditions.

He watched Prissy, the librarian, sweep up the walk in front of Ridgeway's small library. Bernard, the retiring mayor, tidied the bins of vegetables and dry goods displayed outside his mercantile. Folks greeted each other as they moved in an out of the building housing the telegraph and post office.

Buck's voice interrupted his observations. "Alright, Greg. Pony up to the chair." He slapped the backrest of the leather chair with his towel, emphasizing his words.

Standing, Gregory moved from his waiting spot to the barber's chair. As he settled in, he realized he'd been so focused on what was happening outside, he hadn't even noticed the previous patron's exit.

Buck spread a large canvas cape over him, securing it around his neck by doing up the long ties attached to it.

"So, how goes the law keeping?"

"About the same as ever." He couldn't help thinking of Angel as he answered Buck's question, and wondered what she might be doing at the moment. She was a saloon owner; an unorthodox career for a woman. Odds were she was still in bed at this early hour.

"I bet. Heard you arrested our saloon keeper yesterday." Buck used his shears to trim away some of the overgrowth atop his head, and the clipped hairs began to fall down on the shoulders of the cape like dark snowflakes.

He cringed, though he wasn't surprised Buck knew about the incident. In a town as small as Ridgeway, there were no secrets, at least not for long. "I did. She and her trouble-making friends were blocking traffic, not to mention disturbing the peace with all their shouting and carrying on."

That drew a chuckle from Buck. "I gathered as much. One of my customers walked in here claiming to have left his horse and buggy in the middle of the street."

He wanted to shake his head, but refrained so as not to interfere with the haircut. "She went quietly, mostly. Once she was actually in the cell she wouldn't button her lip for nothin'. "

"She's a sassy one, ain't she? Just like the girls back home in Buffalo." Buck often spoke fondly of his hometown back East in New York. "If I hadn't grown accustomed to these mild California winters, I'd move back there."

He recalled his conversation with Angel in the jail, and felt a slight smile creep over his face. "Sassy doesn't begin to cover it. She's stubborn, mouthy, and a shrew. Still, she's smarter than most females I've seen around these parts."

Buck ran a comb through Gregory's hair, and brushed away the loose strands left from the trimming. "Smart females can be a handful. Maybe that's why I'm past forty and still a bachelor. Just haven't found the one worth the trouble yet."

Kianna Alexander

Gregory gave a dismissive wave. "Pshaw. You're probably better off on your own. Women are more trouble than they're worth."

Buck chuckled. "Maybe, but being coupled up has it's benefits, if you get my meaning."

He did. A man had needs, needs that he himself kept tucked away so he could remain focused on his work. "I want a woman like my ma. She's quite, docile, and always there to see to my Papa's needs." Truly, Marie Simmons was the model after which the female race should have been patterned.

"That may be so. But a woman like Angel will keep you young and spry for a good long while. She may be mouthy, but she's a beauty." With the leather strap mounted to the counter pulled taut, Buck began sharpening his straight razor.

"Ain't no disputing that." Gregory leaned back in the chair and let his eyes close.

In his mind, he could see Angel as she'd been yesterday at the jail. He recalled the sparkle in her dark eyes, the way she'd gestured and pointed as she spoke. She'd made it clear that shyness and reservedness were not qualities she possessed. Nothing about her that reminded her of his dear mother, yet her dark beauty intrigued him. A few short years ago, he'd ribbed Noah about being attracted to Valerie. Times were changing, yes, but the change was slow going. A lot of folks still didn't approve of mixing the races.

Noah hadn't let Gregory, or anyone for that matter, dissuade him from pursuing Valerie. Now, more than two years later, Noah happiness could not be denied or ignored. His whole world was his wife and young son, and he'd never seemed more content or fulfilled.

Gregory realized that now, he found himself fascinated by a jewel of the darker race. While he didn't know how to handle it, he did know better than to dismiss it completely because she was a woman of color.

Kianna Alexander

Soon, he felt Buck spreading the cool shaving cream over his face with the soft bristled brush. With smooth, long strokes, Buck moved the razor over his skin, sweeping away the wiry beard he'd grown. "Enough about women. This is a barbershop, where men talk about manly things. So tell me, what's next for Noah's campaign?"

While grateful for the change in topic, he couldn't say he was thrilled to be talking about Noah. The sheriff had been his most trusted friend for years, but lately he seemed so distracted with the election, Gregory rarely even saw him. "I don't know what he's up to. If he's not busy with some political duty or another, he's spending his time at home with Valerie and little Abraham." He didn't begrudge Noah his family or his career, but he did miss his friend.

"Hmm." Buck uttered a contemplative groan as he made a second pass with the razor. "He's got my vote. Can't abide that Nathan Greer, myself. Man's so racist his name oughta be Jim Crow."

Gregory had to agree with his friend's assessment. More than once, he'd been in the saloon and overheard Greer's latest diatribe about how the negro race was inferior to the white race in every way. Greer held much the same low regard for anyone else of color, be they native, or Hispanic, Asian, or otherwise. Anyone who tried to disagree with Greer would be met with his ire, along with another long speech about why Greer's opinion was the only one that was right. Gregory never got into such arguments, because he believed them to be foolish. He'd known Buck five years or more, and he couldn't reconcile the image of the lazy, nary-do-well Negro painted by Greer with the true nature of his hardworking, honest friend. "I don't know who he's expecting will vote for him, with the mean, hateful nonsense he's spouting all over town."

Buck's answering chuckle held no humor, only bitterness. "Oh, some folks will vote for him. Folks that share his opinions about how worthless Negros are." He made a small adjustment to Gregory's sideburns, then tossed the razor into a basin of water and vinegar he kept nearby.

Gregory ran a hand over his newly clean shaven jaw, his brow furrowed. "I just can't believe folks still holding on to that mess in this day and age. The damn war's been over for twenty years now."

Buck didn't look up from wiping the blade of the razor with a clean cloth. "Rational folks know that, but the old Rebs, and the old ways, die hard."

He saw the truth in Buck's words, and while it pained him, he knew there wasn't much he could do to change it. California had never been a slave holding state. Even prior to it's admission to the Union in 1852, when the area was Spanish territory, slavery had not been the law of the land. But from the attitude of some of the folks in town, especially those who migrated West after the devastation visited on their Southern homes by the War Between the States, one wouldn't know that black citizens were essentially equal under the law.

He remembered those days of war. He'd been back home in Sacramento then, just a boy coming of age. No one he knew personally had gone to fight, but he recalled the misty mornings he spent listening to his father read accounts of the battles from the newspaper. He'd heard of the tragedies, such as the massive losses on both sides at the Battle of the Wilderness, and the feats of bravery, such as those performed at Chickamauga by Major General George H. Thomas, revered as the "Rock of Chickamauga." Some of the reports had made he and his brothers cheer boisterously, while others described things so grisly, his mother's face had gone pale and white as milled flour. If he, someone who'd been only a child with no real connection to the war, still felt the gravity of those days, he couldn't imagine how it must have affected someone like Buck.

Buck's dark eyes held sadness. "Lot of my classmates and neighbors fought in the war. Some never came back."

Kianna Alexander

He recognized the melancholy that talking about the war often brought on in Buck. Wanting to lighten the mood, he reached for his wallet. "How much do I owe ya, Buck?"

Buck stood silent for a few moments. Then, he seemed to break free of the memories. Placing the newly cleaned razor in the velvet lined case on his counter, he gave a slight smile. "That'll be three dollars. Same as always."

He handed Buck the payment, then slid out of the chair and stood. "Well, I best be getting out of here. I've got morning patrols to do."

Tucking the money into a the cash drawer built into his counter, Buck nodded. "Good luck out there, friend."

In the doorway, Gregory stopped to place his Stetson atop his head. He touched the brim, looking in Buck's direction. "See you later, Buck."

With that, he stepped out of the barber shop and onto the plank walk outside.

***

Angel sat in a chair inside Lilly's Dress Emporium, half-listening to the conversations happening around her. The shop had closed an hour ago, but she and many of the other women who'd dubbed themselves Crusaders for the Vote were gathered inside. They taken up seats in chairs, on overturned barrels; some even sat on the floor between the dress forms and shelves bursting with Lilly's latest fashionable creations. Lupe had stayed behind to work the bar at the saloon in order to let Angel attend the meeting, and she'd slipped away only a few minutes ago.

Lilly Benigno, proprietor of the shop, stood atop a crate and called the women to order. "Good Evening, ladies. As you know, the Ridgeway Tribune has been reporting on our activities as we agitate for our voting rights. Catherine McCormack tells me that her husband, our illustrious journalist, has even been submitting our news to the

Associated Press."

Chatter rose among the women on the heels of that announcement. Angel smiled, pleased to hear that news of their efforts was being spread beyond the borders of their small town.

Lilly extracted a folded paper from beneath her arm, and continued. "I'd like you all to hear what was printed in today's San Francisco Chronicle about us, written by a Mr. John T. West. And I quote, 'The talk of suffrage has been around for a long time, with little progress. However, that hasn't discouraged a group of particularly demanding females, in the small enclave of Ridgeway, near Oakland, from abandoning their duties of washing, cooking, and tending the home in favor of protests and marches that disrupt traffic and create problems for their men-folk.' Can you believe that?"

Angel's brow furrowed, and she raised her voice to speak. "Why, that's a male superior view if ever I heard one. McCormack always reports the story objectively. How could that brigand twist the story to make us sound like a bunch of nary-do-wells?"

Prissy Parker, the town's librarian, scoffed. "It seems this Mr. West has his own agenda in mind, and means to perpetrate it, even if it means insulting us."

With a shake of her head, Angel sighed. If this Mr. West couldn't keep his personal opinions separate from his work, then journalism wasn't the field for him. His antiquated attitudes were a detriment to his ability to report the news as it was, rather than as he saw it. She'd love to meet this Mr. West, and give a good sized piece of her mind. For every woman like her, working hard to gain her rights, there were two or three stubborn, bull headed men like him trying to undermine her efforts. She wondered what men thought would happen if they just gave in and let women be equal citizens. What were they so afraid of?

As if giving voice to her thoughts, Lilly proclaimed, "It's as if men think that if they give us any rights, we'll immediately overthrow the government and banish them all to work camps in some dreadful place. I just can't make heads or tails of it."

Prissy quipped, "Or maybe their simply afraid they'll be forced to mend their own damn shirts, or heaven forbid, cook for themselves."

A few chuckles met that flip remark. Prissy could always be counted on to call it as she saw it.

Lilly sighed. "It's a shame, really. And what makes it worse is that we couldn't even get the commitment of all the women here in Ridgeway. Some of them refused to join us because they don't care about political matters, and others refused to be an integrated group."

Angel looked around at the women gathered in the shop. There were women of many races and backgrounds present, but the truth of Lilly's words still stung. Some of the ladies of this town just didn't give a damn, and she could almost understand that. What she couldn't understand was the women who turned their noses up at the idea of marching alongside their counterparts of other races, or those who didn't have enough money or social standing to meet their high standards. If it weren't for those foolish prejudices, the Crusaders would likely number in the hundreds instead of the forty or so currently serving.

From among the women, someone asked, "What are we going to do now?"

Lilly, her jaw set, raised her fist. "I'll tell you what we're going to do. We're going to keep right on protesting until we get our rights."

Angel jumped to her feet. "Lilly's right. I've already survived being arrested and thrown in jail. I say we give 'em hell till they give in!"

Even the usually stoic Prudence Emerson, wife of the town's minister, seemed riled. "The men of this town owe us! We've cooked their meals, scrubbed their floors, and borne their babes. They are gonna do right by us, whether they like it or not!"

A rousing burst of cheering and applause filled the dress shop.

Angel joined in the revelry, a smile spreading across her face. She imagined Mr. San Francisco Reporter would be none too pleased to learn that his snide article had only encouraged the "demanding women" of Ridgeway to redouble their efforts. "And if they don't like it, tell them to direct their complaints to Mr. John T. West, care of the San Francisco Chronicle!"

The women spent a little while formulating their strategy for the next protest, before saying their goodbyes, and parting ways.

Later, with a dampened cloth in her grasp, Angel wiped down the bar surface at night's end. The midnight hour neared, and she was bone-tired from what had proven to be an exceptionally busy Tuesday evening at the Crazy Eights. Sweeping the remnant of peanut shells and popcorn hulls into the refuse bin at her feet, she blew a lock of hair out of her face. From the shelf below the counter, she grabbed the tin of polish she used to maintain the bar's wooden surface, then set to work polishing it.

While she worked the polish into the grain of the hand carved mahogany, she thought of Gary Greenfield, the previous owner. He'd commissioned a craftsman from San Francisco make the counter, and had lovingly preserved it for the two decades he'd run the place. Just a few months ago, Mr. Greenfield had retired to Los Angeles, leaving the ownership of the saloon to her, his most trusted employee. Greenfield, over twenty five years her senior, had always treated her with kindness and respect, and she had a very high regard for him. She thought of him in an almost paternal sense; he'd been the only such figure to ever enter her life. While she missed him dearly, she didn't begrudge him his well-earned retirement, and they kept in contact through letters and the occasional telegraph.

"Angel? Angel, are you still up?" The familiar voice came from her apartment, built onto the rear of the saloon.

Hearing her aunt's call, she quickly finished her task. "Yes, Aunt Myrna. Do you need something?"

"Yes, I need you to go to bed and get some sleep!" came the reply.

With a chuckle, she set the rag and polish aside. Her aunt could be rather insistent at times, but she knew Myrna Lane Corcoran loved her fiercely, and the feeling was mutual. So, she called back, "Yes, Ma'am." Making sure all the lanterns on the bar, the tables, and the window ledges were doused, she dusted her hands off on her denims and strolled through the door to her apartment.

The door led to a short corridor, on the end of which was a second door that opened into the apartment. Due to the occasional lost visitor to town, or confused patron who'd imbibed too much, that door was kept bolted. Unlocking the door with the key hanging around her neck, she entered and closed the door behind her, throwing the latch to secure it.

The owner's apartment was not palatial by any stretch, but was certainly larger than any room to let in town. Even the cabin she'd lived in before, on the edge of a neighboring town, had not been much larger. One large room served as kitchen and parlor, while two smaller rooms were her bedroom and the bathing room. Aside from the convenience of living just steps away from her business, the bathing room, with it's fancy plumbing system and claw footed bathtub was her favorite part of living here.

Opposite her room, on the far end of the parlor, Myrna had erected an ornate bamboo screen. The screen had been a souvenir from her younger days, when she'd acted in a production company that toured up and down the Pacific coast. She'd picked the screen up on a trip to Chinatown in San Francisco, and now it served to separate her private space from the rest of the area.

Now, Angel went to the screen and peeked around it. Her aunt reclined on her low, cot-like bed, her silver hair wrapped in the blue silk scarf she wore to protect it at night. She sat propped against her many pillows, copper-rimmed reading glasses perched on the end of her nose, with a open book on her lap. The Lane family quilt, sewn from the scraps of baby clothes, wedding gowns, and other significant pieces of fabric from the family's history, was draped over the lower half of her body.

Myrna looked up from her reading, offered a soft smile. "Good, child. So you're finally going to bed?"

"Yes ma'am." She leaned down to kiss her aunt's brow. "What are you reading?"

"The Canterbury Tales. Written by a Geoffrey Chaucer. A bit dreadful and crass in places, but still not a bad read."

"Ah." She knew of her aunt's love of literature from all over the world, and was not surprised to find her reading at this, or any hour.

"So, what happened today while you were incarcerated?"

The question caught Angel by surprise, and she blinked. "Well, not much. I did try to sway Gregory to our side, though. I'm not sure I succeeded, but at least I showed him not all females are daft doxies whose interests don't extend beyond the latest designs in the Godey's Ladies Book."

Her aunt's expression changed, a silver eyebrow arched. "Gregory, is that the deputy's first name? I never knew it. When did the two of you become so informal?"

She felt warmth creeping into her face. "Today, I suppose. He asked me to call him that."

Myrna said nothing, but offered a knowing smile.

Aware of her aunt's thoughts, she shook her head. "Now, Aunt Myrna. Don't start your mental matchmaking. I'm a saloon owner- the deputy and I are not suited."

The older woman gave a soft sigh. "Yes, yes, if you say so. You know the only two things I wish to do before I leave this life are to cast a ballot, and to see you married. Don't begrudge an old woman her hopes."

With a half smile, she touched her aunt's cheek. She loved her mother's elder sister with all her heart, and knew her meddling to be well meaning. "I'm going to bed."

"Sure you are." Myrna looked down at the volume, turned the page. "As soon as I finish 'The Wife of Bath's Tale,', I'm off to sleep myself. Goodnight, dear."

"Goodnight, Auntie." She walked around the screen and left her aunt to her reading. In the bathing room, she washed her face in the basin and glanced at the tub. As much as she wanted to enjoy a hot soak, her tired body cried out for the bed.

That isn't all I'm crying out for. The thought of Gregory met her as soon as she slipped beneath the covers. He was so handsome, it almost hurt her eyes to look at him. Dark hair grazing his neck, the shadowy beard along his strong jaw, and the assessing, coal black eyes. The brief contact of their bodies when he'd freed her from the cell earlier had sent sparks shooting through her. Heat seemed to radiate from every pore of his well-muscled body. It was why she'd sent Lupe around to pay her fines; she wasn't sure she could keep control of her faculties if she had to be in his overwhelming presence twice in the same day.

A yawn escaped her, and she rolled over onto her side. The night breeze lifted the ends of her white lace curtains, and the chill made her get up to close the swinging pane of glass. That done, she slipped back beneath the bedding atop her bed, and closed her eyes.

Before sleep could claim her, her aunt's laughter broke the silence.

"Angel! Come and read this part, it's hilarious!"

Shaking her head, she dragged her tired body from the bed and went to see what her aunt wanted to show her.

Chapter 3

The following afternoon, Angel stood behind the saloon's bar, going over the alcohol inventory with Joel, the man who came by to take orders for the distillery over in Oakland.

"So I'll need another case of whiskey, a case of rum, and about five bottles of vodka, please." She looked up from the small notebook she used to tally her liquor orders, and found the squat little fellow staring, as was his way, at her bosom. She supposed some of it had to do with his lack of height, but he was mostly just a pervert in her mind.

Joel noted her request, then tucked away his black leather bound ledger. His gaze rose, but still focused on her chest. "Yes, Miss Lane. No problem."

She wrinkled her nose in disgust, crossed her arms over her chest to block his view. "Joel, unless you expect my bosom to produce a wallet and pay for this, you'd best start looking me in the eye."

His beady eyes shifted, then lowered. "Sorry, Miss Lane. Plainspoken as always, I see." He made haste to jot her a receipt on one of the pages of his book, then ripped it out and handed it to her.

She took the paper, slipping it into the pocket of her denims. "I run a saloon, for Pete's sake. I gave up sweet words and fancy talk long ago. Have a good day, Joel."

The little man grabbed up his hat and case, and exited.

Not long after he left, Lupe entered for her shift. Wearing her barmaid's uniform of white blouse, red vest, and fitted black trousers, she'd bound her long black hair in a low bun. In the three years that Lupe and she Angel had tended the bar at the Crazy Eights side by side, they'd become good friends. "Just saw Joel hitching his wagon. Has he been here holding a conversation with your bosoms again?"

Chuckling, Angel nodded. She was amazed that even though Joel had been coordinating her liquor orders for months, he never seemed to tire of looking down her blouse. "Sure has. The man's got no manners."

Lupe echoed her laugh as she passed the upright piano sitting near the door. The sound of the pointed heels of her tall black boots echoed on the hardwood floors as she navigated the maze of tables and eased behind the bar. There, she stashed her handbag on a low shelf beneath the counter, and grabbed up her polish cloth and a glass from the rack. "They oughta hire a lady to take the orders. Give her a gun to take care of anybody who means her harm."

She agreed with Lupe, but still shook her head. "That ain't never gonna happen. You know how men are. They think we're too dumb to do much of anything that don't involve cooking, cleaning, or birthing and raising their babies."

Running the rag over a tall pilsner, Lupe sighed. "You're right, men don't think much of us. Like they're so smart. They get a sniff of perfume, or a look at our bosoms, and can't even hardly function." She jabbed a finger in the air, gesturing toward Angel's outfit.

Looking down at the ruffled, off the shoulder collar of her lavender blouse, she shrugged. "I don't dress for those fool men, or for anybody else. I just wear what I like. Those damn gowns and corsets are just too tight and uncomfortable for a woman running a business."

Lupe moved on to the next glass, shining it until it sparkled in the sunlight. "Agreed. I have a hard enough time moving about in this vest." She adjusted the jet buttons running down the center with a smirk.

Angel pulled out her uncle's old pocket watch from her denims, yet another thing that made the men of town call her 'unorthodox'. She made note of the time. "Open up the bar in about fifteen minutes, Lupe."

The barmaid nodded as she tucked the last glass back into the rack. "Will do."

Intent on making a few final preparations for the saloon's opening, Angel drifted away from the counter and moved out into the mass of tables. She used the cloth she kept tucked in her waistband to dust a few smudges off the wooden surfaces of the tables and chairs, made sure the spittoon was emptied and clean, and check the oil lamps set on each table to make sure their fuel levels were right.

At the last table, closest to the bar, she found a mysterious sticky, dark spot. Her brow furrowed, as she assumed it to be a bit of chewing tobacco, dribbled there by one of her patrons. Groaning, she whipped out her cloth again and began scrubbing the spot.

She was so engrossed in getting rid of the nasty stain that she didn't notice anyone entering the saloon. The first indication she had of Deputy Simmons's presence was the smell of him. The masculine scent of leather and cigar smoke filled her nostrils and she was nearly overcome. She didn't even have to look up to identify him, or to know that he stood mere feet from her.

"Evenin', Miss Lane." The deep timbre of his voice affected her, vibrating through her very being as he spoke. He'd removed his tan Stetson upon entering the saloon, and had it in one hand, resting on his hip. The absence of his hat revealed his raven dark locks. His hair was no longer touching the base of his neck, but had been freshly trimmed into a neater cut. Gone was the shadowy beard, allowing her the full experience of his handsome, angular face.

She ceased her scrubbing, and straightened up to her full height, which was still at least five inches less than his. As she angled her neck to look into his watchful black eyes, she felt her pulse quickening. "Evenin', Deputy."

He took another step closer, his wide, muscular frame obstructing her view of the saloon's interior. "Now, now. I already know you're a troublemaker; no need to be so formal. Call me Greg, like I said before." His tone held humor, as if he amused himself.

She recognized his attempt at goading her, and that helped to break the trance he'd put her under. Placing a hand to her chest and feigning offense, she released a dramatic sigh. "Honestly, Greg. I'm not a troublemaker. Just trying to get my message heard."

He nodded his head, gave her a small smile of appeasement. "Sure, sure. Just remember not to block traffic and you can spout your nonsense all over town if you like." He gave her a wink, and sidled over to the bar, taking up residence on one of the stools.

She rolled her eyes. He displayed the typical male point of view, and she wondered if they would ever abandon their wrongheaded way of thinking. Even though he annoyed her, she couldn't help admiring the sight of his denim-clad behind, perched on the brown leather padded seat of the stool he occupied. He might be arrogant, and even a bit insufferable, but his rear end was so nice, it almost made up for it.

Almost.

Lupe, who'd been silently wiping the same area of the bar from the moment the deputy strode in, plastered on a smile. "Howdy, Deputy. What's your pleasure?"

Laying his Stetson on the bar's top, he gave her a nod of greeting. "Howdy, Lupe. Get me a sarsaparilla, if you please. Duty tonight. Wouldn't want to be seen about with a brick in my hat."

"Comin' right up." Lupe filled a glass with the dark, bubbly liquid from the tap behind the bar, then slid the glass in his direction.

He caught it deftly, stopping its slide with the open palm of his large hand.

Angel could see the invitation in Lupe's smile, and she felt a twinge of irritation. She drew a deep breath, and mused on where the negative feelings could be coming from. She couldn't really blame Lupe for noticing how handsome the deputy was. Every sighted woman between here and Sacramento would probably agree that he was easy on the eyes. Beyond that, she had no claims on him, and therefore no right to be upset. Feeling she was thinking entirely too hard about a man, especially one with such backward views, she settled onto a stool next to him.

He'd downed most of the sarsaparilla, and was now looking at a notebook of some kind, which he'd opened and placed in front of him on the bar.

Curious, she leaned a bit closer, but found she couldn't make out the handwritten notes scribbled in the book. "What's that book, Greg?"

"We use it to keep up with our arrest records. Helps us point out repeat offenders, keep up with their whereabouts, and all that." He ran his finger over the page, then shut the book and tucked it away.

Hearing his explanation got her to thinking about what had happened the other day. "Is my name in there? Do I have a record now?"

He chuckled. "Yes. I did have to arrest you, so you're listed in it. As of now, though, we have no reason to believe you'll be a repeat offender."

She folded her arms over her chest. "You mean to tell me I've got a criminal record, just because I stood up for what I believe in, for what's right?"

"That's about the balance of it. But I certainly wouldn't say it's 'right' to cause such a disruption to the town, especially in the name of such a silly cause."

She tried, without success, to keep the incredulity out of her voice. "Are you serious? After everything we spoke about, you still don't believe women should have the right to vote?"

His broad shoulders lifted in a shrug. "Sorry, Angel, but I don't. It's true enough that you know just about everything there is to know about politics, on the local and national levels. Still, I don't think other women can boast such knowledge. And even if they could, who's to say it would make a difference?"

Every little short hair on the back of Angel's neck stood on end.

As if sensing her ire, Lupe dropped her rag and disappeared into the storage room directly behind the bar's mirrored liquor shelf.

Before she could stop herself, Angel hopped down from the bar stool and slid it aside, so she could stand very close to Greg. Of it's own accord, her index finger stretched out, bisecting the thin swath of air between her face and his shoulder. "So the article I read in this morning's paper was right about you, huh? Still dead set against women being treated as equal citizens."

He rolled his eyes. "McCormack baited me. I didn't read his damn article, but you knew how I felt before."

"You men just think you're some pumpkins, don't you. I'm not going to go for anymore of this foolishness. Women are equal to men. We're just as smart, just as capable, and just as worthy of rights as you and your testosterone driven contingent."

His jaw took on a tight set as he swallowed the last of his drink. He set the glass down, and he swiveled on the bar stool to pierce her with his gaze. "Is that so, Miss Lane?"

"It sure as hell is! And I know plenty of folks who'd even say women are better than men. Some of y'all are so short on sense you couldn't beat a horse in a spelling contest."

His gaze hardened with anger, he wrapped his hand around her pointing finger and tugged it down. "First off, get that little finger outta my face. I'm still the law around here. And second off, women and men ain't equal. You're seven by nine to us, and you'd best work on accepting your natural place."

She snatched her finger from his grasp, her hands crumpling into fists at her sides. Her next words erupted in an outraged shout. "MY NATURAL PLACE!"

If he was put off by her yelling, he didn't let on. "That's right, your natural place. My dear mother has gotten great joy out of caring for her menfolk, me, my two brothers, Pa, my uncle, and my Grandpa. It's hard work, sure, but there's respect to be had from hard work."

She narrowed her eyes. "Ha! You may love your mama but there ain't no way you respect her. If you did you wouldn't be holding on to these fool notions that women are worthless if they ain't doing your bidding!"

He groaned. "Cool down your pucker, I didn't say that!"

"I doesn't matter that you didn't say it. Your attitude is plain to see. I don't reckon you ever told your mama that despite all her 'hard work', you don't think she's fit to be your equal under the law."

His dark eyes flashed with something akin to guilt, but it was quickly replaced with indignation. "Alright now, enough of this."

She leaned in close to him. "No. It won't be enough until you change your fool mind."

"I'm right, and there ain't no need for me to change!"

"Balderdash! If you weren't the law 'round here I'd knock you right off that stool!"

He leaned closer, so close their noses almost touched. "Well I am the law, so quit having a conniption fit, and get out of my face!"

"Ugh!"

A moment after the sound of disgust left her lips, she felt a twinge. For a second she fought like hell to contain the urge.

Then she crushed her mouth against his.

He reacted with surprise, but didn't push her away. Soon their lips were melting together as the kiss became earnest, real. His tongue brushed her bottom lip, and her whole body trembled.

He ended the kiss, abruptly pulling away as if he'd suddenly come to his senses. "What in Sam Hill are you about? One minute you're cursing me, and next you kiss me?"

She drew a deep breath, embarrassment heating her cheeks. "Well, it was either kiss you or cuff you, so I did what I had to do to stay outta jail."

He shook his head, dark eyes wide with confusion. "You're plumb crazy, woman."

She propped her fists on her hips, her body still tingling from their brief kiss. "That might be so, but this is my place. So just pay up for the drink and skedaddle, why don't you."

"Gladly." He tossed a half eagle on the counter, grabbed up his hat, and got down from the stool.

She watched his walk away. At the door, he stuck his Stetson atop his head. With one last, cutting look, he stepped out into the late afternoon sunshine, and disappeared.

It was then that Angel noticed the three men seated at the table nearest the piano. She didn't recognize any of them, but that wasn't uncommon in her establishment.

Three sets of curious male eyes were trained on her, and she could feel her cheeks redden as they silently assessed her.

Steeling herself, she nodded to them. "Evenin', gentlemen. Welcome to the Crazy Eights."

She turned and started to yell for Lupe, but the barmaid stuck her head out from the storage closet door. "Is he gone? Are you done scolding him?"

She closed her eyes, touched her aching temple. "Lupe, just serve our customers, will ya?"

Once she knew her patrons would be taken care of, she left the main room to escape to her apartment.

***

Around the supper hour, Gregory sat behind the desk in

the sheriff's office. Before him on the polished wood surface sat the empty bowl that had held his evening meal. He'd polished off a serving of Ruby's famous beef stew, as well as the two biscuits that had come with it. Now, as he took a draw from the tumbler of lemonade, he realized that eating had banished the growling of his stomach, but hadn't really cooled his anger.

The encounter with Angel at the saloon still pestered him, like a worrisome fly buzzing in his ear. She was beautiful, that much was true. But she was far too bossy, and opinionated for his tastes. At every turn, she seemed to enjoy contradicting him, fussing at him, or otherwise bedeviling him. He preferred elegant, docile women; women like his mother, whom he'd never heard say a cross word to any of the men in his family. Even when he and his brother were young boys, making mischief at every opportunity, she'd always spoken to them with patience and love in her voice. Why couldn't Angel be more like that? Why did she insist on being a thorn in his side?

As he mulled over the questions, the door swung open. Noah strode in, removing his hat as he crossed the threshold. "Hey, Greg. What's the matter with you? You look like you've been chewing rocks."

Gregory tried to release the tension he knew was displayed on his face, but the best he could muster was a weak, half smile. "Evenin', Noah. Chewing rocks might've been more pleasant than tangling with some ornery, hardheaded woman."

Noah gave a chuckle, taking a moment to prop the door open with the small wedge of wood they kept for that purpose. "Well, well. I'm guessing you and Angel May have crossed paths again." He leaned back against the wall, folding his arms over his chest.

Gregory looked at his friend's amused expression and shook his head. "Yes, and don't look so pleased about it. I can't even enjoy a sarsaparilla at the bar without her shouting and carrying on about that women's right to vote foolishness."

The sheriff scoffed. "Foolishness, eh? Better not let my Val hear you say that. She'd box your ears for sure, and I wouldn't stop her, neither."

"You saying you think women ought to have the vote?"

"Sure, I don't see no good reason they shouldn't."

He leaned forward in his chair, his voice taking on a conciliatory tone. "Come on now, Noah. Ain't nobody here but you and me. This ain't no campaign speech, you can tell me the truth."

Noah's brow furrowed. "I am telling you the truth. If women want to vote, I say we let them. And that's the God's honest truth as I see it."

"Why in Sam Hill would you want women to vote?"

"Why are you so set against it? Times are changing, Greg. Women are doctors, lawyers, some are even mayors. There are plenty of towns where the women outnumber the men."

"Well, that ain't the case in Ridgeway. The women here are too busy making trouble when they ought to be tending to their own affairs."

Noah said nothing, just gave him a look.

"Letting them vote is just asking for more trouble."

Noah shook his head. "Looks like we just don't agree on this, so you're welcome to vote for the other guy if you want." He gave a wink.

Gregory scratched his chin, and decided to let the matter drop. "What are you doing here, anyhow? You haven't worked a late shift since you married Miss Valerie."

"Not working this evening, either. Didn't Thaddeus tell you about the interview at change of shift?"

His eyebrow cocked. "Thaddeus didn't say anything to me, just rushed out of here. What interview?"

Noah eased over to the chair in front of the desk and sat down, rolling his eyes. "That boy ain't got much in the way of short term memory. Anyway, Kyle is coming by this evening to interview us for the Tribune."

Gregory knew the newspaperman would want to hear from Noah, since he was running in the mayor's race. But he couldn't guess what Kyle expected him to contribute. "Why am I being interviewed? I'm not in this race."

"Kyle knows we have opposing views on the whole women's voting issue. Maybe he's wanting to write about that, but I don't really know."

He groaned. "Good grief. I wish you'd told me about this."

Noah chuckled. "I knew you'd run for the hills. But I did ask Thad to pass the word."

Gregory ran a hand over his hair. If the newspaperman was already coming, there was no way to get out of it now. So he steeled himself as best he could. In a town like Ridgeway, there wasn't an abundance of excitement, at least not since the Bitters gang had terrorized the area a few years ago. As annoyed as he was, he much preferred being interviewed to having actual crime filling the pages of the Tribune, and he'd bet good coin that the citizens of town would agree.

He and Noah spoke for a few moments, and he listened with a smile as Noah rambled on about his son, Abraham. Little Abe was approaching five years old, and Noah never lacked for stories of the boy's latest discovery or accomplishment. Noah was going on about how good Abe was at writing his name on a slate when the newspaperman strode in.

Dressed in dark slacks, a crisp white shirt, and a dark blue vest, Kyle McCormack eased into the office with the same confident air he displayed everywhere. He wore the black bowler hat he rarely removed, and this time was no exception. Beneath the hat, a few strands of dark red hair peeked out. His green eyes held curiosity and a bit of humor. "Good evening, gentleman. I'm so glad you could take time out to speak with me." The sharp accent of his

Boston upbringing punctuated his words.

Gregory and Noah each shook his extended hand, then Gregory rose from the seat behind the desk. "I'll fetch an extra chair for you, McCormack."

Kyle raised his hand. "That won't be necessary. I prefer to stand, and besides, I don't want to monopolize too much of you gentleman's time."

Gregory retook his seat, a bit tickled by Kyle's tendency toward fancy words like 'monopolize.' Keeping that to himself, he settled in to see what the interview would bring.

At first, most of Kyle's questions were directed at Noah. As he queried him about his stance on this issue or that, Kyle recorded every response on the small pad of of paper he'd extracted from his vest pocket. Then, looking up from the pad, Kyle fixed his eyes directly on Gregory. "So, Deputy Simmons. I understand you're opposed to the female citizens of Ridgeway casting their votes. May I ask why?"

He cringed. The reporter shot from the hip. "McCormack, are you baiting me into some kind of argument here? What are you about?"

Kyle wrinkled his nose. "No, sir. I'm a journalist, and I remain objective on every subject. I have no opinion one way or the other- but I'm still interested in hearing your side of things. I believe the people of town are interested as well, since you'll be sheriff if Noah wins the mayor's seat."

Gregory ran a hand over his damp brow. McCormack's words pointed to an inconvenient truth- even though he wasn't running in the mayor's race, he was in a campaign of sorts. The people of town had to be comfortable with him, if he were to have any success as a full fledged sheriff. "I don't have much to say on the matter. I simply believe a woman's time and attention is better spent on other affairs."

McCormack jotted on the pad. "By 'other affairs,' I assume you mean domestic tasks; cooking, cleaning, rearing children?"

While the newspaper man claimed objectivity, there was something in his tone that got Gregory's dander up. "Now wait just a minute. I didn't say..."

Noah stuck up his hand, as if sensing his deputy's ire. "Now, now McCormack. That'll be enough hounding my deputy, he's not in this race. What matters is if I'm elected, I will extend voting rights to all citizens of Ridgeway. That, you can print, in bold type if you like."

McCormack cleared his throat and ceased his scribbling. Closing the small pad, he inserted it and his pencil back in the pocket of his vest. "That'll be all for now, gentleman. Have a pleasant evening."

The reporter smiled, touched the brim of his bowler, and exited through the open door.

Noah stood then, running a hand through his blonde locks before replacing his Stetson. "Sorry, Gregory. I didn't know he'd be so irritating."

Gregory nodded. "It's alright. Just don't be volunteering me for any more interviews."

"Understood. Well, I'm headed home to see Val and Abe. Send around a note if you need anything." Noah strode out.

Gregory sat back in the chair, feeling his brow furrowed. He couldn't quite identify what had just happened, but he just knew that when the morning edition came out tomorrow, there was bound to be trouble.

His hunch was correct. When he strolled by the newspaper office the next day and picked up a copy, the headline on the front page read, "Mayoral Candidate Supports Suffrage, Potential Sheriff Says No."

With a groan, he tossed the paper into the nearest rubbish bin, and kept walking.

Chapter 4

Angel moved along the back side of the bar, collecting the eagles and assorted coins that had been left as tips, and placed them in the jar on the shelf below. Moving the used glasses to the basin to be washed, she grabbed the cloth hooked to the waist of her denims and began wiping the bar down. It was just past the six o'clock hour, and as more of the men in Ridgeway and the surrounding areas got off work for the day, the saloon was bound to get a bumper crop of customers.

Glancing at her reflection in the mirrored shelves holding her bottles of liquor, she tucked a few loose hairs back into her low bun. She'd put on a new blouse today, this one light blue with a ruffled collar that bared her shoulders and collarbone. Seeing that she'd managed to keep it clean and free from rips thus far pleased her. Serving drinks and keeping the place clean all day often led to her damaging her garments. That was why she preferred denims and blouses over the gowns and skirts most women wore. Those cumbersome, flimsy things just didn't jibe with her lifestyle.

She turned away from her reflection and set about cleaning the glasses. Since Lupe had gone to Oakland to see about an ill friend, she'd be working the bar alone tonight. Efficiency would be a top priority.

She was drying glasses when a man she didn't recognize entered through the swinging doors. She smiled, offering a customary greeting. "Welcome to the Crazy Eights."

He gave her a nod, removing his flat brimmed hat. He was an average size fellow in a black vest, blue work shirt, denims and boots. He had ruddy face, framed by dark blonde hair.

His eyes were on her, but had obviously settled much

lower than her face.

She ignored him, being accustomed to such scrutiny from the men who patronized her establishment.

He moved inside the saloon, and sat a a table near the door.

Since he didn't appear to be in any sort of hurry, she kept drying and shining the glasses. "I'll be over shortly to take your order."

He said nothing, but continued leering at her.

The doors swung open again, and this time, Gregory strode in.

She rolled her eyes as he beat his path straight to the bar.

"Evenin', Angel." He took a seat on the stool nearest to where she stood.

She barely looked up. "Deputy. What can I get you?"

"Sarsaparilla. Oh, and you could look like you appreciate my business, if it's not too much trouble."

She sighed, but looked up anyway. His dark, piercing eyes were waiting.

Those damn eyes of his. They made her want to let her guard down, and reveal the soft places inside her soul. As their gazes locked, she felt her lips lift into a smile. "How's that?"

He chuckled. "It's a mighty poor looking smile but it'll do."

That made her chuckle as well. Shaking her head, she reached for a glass. "I'll get you your damned sarsaparilla."

She filled the glass from the tapped barrel on one of the shelves and slid it his way.

The stranger at the table in the back spoke up. "Hey, barmaid. How 'bout some service?"

Angel nodded to Gregory, then eased around the bar and strolled over to the table where the man sat. "Evenin. What can I get you?"

The man smiled, showing of a row of yellow, tobacco stained teeth. His eyes raked over her body like talons. "First thing you can get me is a big helping of you, sweet cheeks."

Frowning, Angel shook her head. "Hold on now, Mister. I don't run that kind of place."

He sat back in his chair, balancing it on the two rear legs, and winked. "Come on now. This is a saloon, ain't it? How you expect to make any money without a few working girls?"

Her anger rose with each passing second, but she strove for professionalism. "Like I said, Mister, we don't do that here. You want a drink, or not?"

"A tall drink of you, sweet cheeks." He lifted his hand and slapped her bottom, hard. The sound reverberated through the nearly empty saloon.

That tore it.

Angel's eyes narrowed, and her vision glowed red.

At the bar, Gregory jumped up from his stool. "Hold on, now."

Before the deputy could make it across the room, Angel balled her fist and drew back. She let loose a punch that hit the man square in his eye. He yowled in pain as the blow sent him and his chair crashing to the floor.

She stood over the cursing, angry man and gave him a smile laced with venom. "This ain't no whorehouse, Mister. You'll do well to remember that."

Gregory appeared beside her, looked down at the man lying on the wooden floor, and whistled. "I'd offer my assistance, but I don't think you need it."

Angel folded her arms over her chest. "Jackass."

Gregory helped the man get up and right the chair. Once the man was on his feet, the deputy posed a question. "Look, I'm deputy sheriff here, and if you want to press charges against Miss Lane, I can..."

The man squinted at Gregory through his good eye. "Hell no, I ain't pressing no charges. It was just a lucky punch. No lady never got the best of me before and it won't happen again!" That said, he grabbed up his hat and shuffled out the way he'd come in.

Once he'd left, Angel returned to the bar. Parts of her were still seething from the encounter, but it had felt damn good to put the jackass in his place."Good riddance, I say."

Gregory returned to his stool and his half finished sarsaparilla. "You're pretty impressive, Angel May."

Looking in his direction, she furrowed her brow. "How's that?"

"Never known a woman who could run a business, keep up with politics, and knock a grown man over like that." He took a draw from his glass. "Yep. Pretty damn impressive."

Hearing him speak of her that way, she smiled. She rested her elbows on the bar, and leaned toward him."Thank you. That's high praise, I reckon."

Their eyes met again, and this time their gazes connected and held.

A few silent beats passed. She could feel her heart rate quicken as the dark pools enraptured her.

"If you don't want me to kiss you, Angel May, now's the time to stop me."

His gruffly spoken words seemed to vibrate through her entire body. Her eyes drifted to his full lips, and she heard herself say softly, "I don't object."

He leaned into her, his large hand reaching out to capture her hair as their lips touched.

This wasn't like then angry kiss she'd given him before. This was much sweeter. She reveled in the feeling of his tongue grazing over her lips and the corners of her mouth, beckoning her to open to him. When she did, and his tongue slipped inside, the passion sparking between them bloomed like a rose opening to the sun. Her hair came loose, but she didn't care as the kiss deepened. He laced his hands into her loose locks, his fingertips massaging her scalp, and a stream of heat radiated from his touch through her entire body.

Only the sound of someone clearing their throat drew her back to reality. Reluctantly, she drew away, and turned to see her aunt Myrna standing by the door to the apartment.

Aided by her mahogany cane, Myrna slowly made her way toward them. "Evenin', Deputy."

Looking altogether uncomfortable, he returned her greeting. "Mrs. Corcoran."

Myrna's brow lifted, the aged face showing a hint of humor. "I came to check on my dear niece, because I knew she'd be working alone tonight. Or at least, that's what I was told."

Angel felt the heat fill her cheeks. Even though she picked up on the humor in her aunt's statement, she couldn't help feeling like a child caught stealing candy. "I'm fine, Aunt Myrna."

"Oh, I can see that, dear." With a wink, the older woman turned and went back through the door to the apartment.

She watched her aunt depart, then turned back to him. "Goodness. I'm thoroughly embarrassed."

He shook his head, a smile creeping over his face. "Don't be. I'm the one who started it...this time."

Hearing him refer to their previous kiss make her cheeks feel even hotter. "Just be glad I kissed you that day instead of socking you like I wanted to."

"I am glad. Especially after the way you laid that fellow out today."

She rolled her eyes, gave him a playful punch in the shoulder. "You think this is all so funny. But now that my aunt's seen you kissing me, she'll expect us to be courting. Nothing she wants more than to see me married off." She cringed, wishing she could take back those last few words. What in the world has possessed her to tell him that?

Nonplussed, he quipped, "I wasn't kissing you. We were kissing each other. And what's wrong with that?"

She shrugged. "What's wrong us kissing? Nothing, I suppose. We're both adults."

"No. I mean, what's wrong with us courting?"

Round eyed, she stared at him. "Have you taken leave of

your good sense?"

Now he shrugged. "Maybe, but I want you."

"You don't want to court me."

He inclined his head. "And why not?"

"What kind of fool question is that? You said yourself that I'm bossy and opinionated, and I ought to be tending to so called 'female affairs' rather than agitating for the vote."

"Yeah, I did say that. But what if I changed my mind?"

"About women voting?"

"No. About you."

He fixed her with a gaze so intense, she had to look away.

"Gregory..."

He grabbed hold of her hand, clasped in both of his atop the polished surface of the bar. "I'm not promising I'll come around to your way of thinking, Angel. But I am promising that if you'll have me, I'll treat you like the treasure you are."

A sigh escaped her lips. She had to admit that she'd enjoyed his kisses, and that even now, the contact of his hands sent the shivers up and down her arm. On matters of principle, she couldn't be more at odds with him. But when it came to this strange, unnamed thing sparking between them, she felt her soul opening up to him. When he was near, her body reacted to his presence as if they were predestined to be close to one another.

He gave her hand a gentle squeeze. "What do you say, Angel? Will you let me court you?"

***

Gregory held fast to Angel's hand, and waited. He'd wait all night if he had to; his shift at the sheriff's office was over for the day. He had nothing but time on his hands, and he was determined to make her his.

He understood her hesitance. Hell, just yesterday, he'd been complaining to Noah about how difficult and hardheaded she was. But after what he'd seen today, he'd evaluated the sum total of everything he knew about Angel, and the qualities she possessed. He'd always known she was beautiful. From the moment he'd laid eyes on her years ago, he'd seen that. That rich dark hair, the sparkling brown eyes, the full bosom and shapely hips bared to his gaze by the denims she insisted on wearing were all signs of her physical beauty.

Since the day he'd arrested her, though, he'd discovered so much more about the person she was. What lay beneath the lovely surface was a complex woman, one he wanted to claim. It was as crazy a notion as had ever entered his mind, but he wanted her, and his desire could no longer be denied.

She blew out a long, slow breath. "If I agree to this fool arrangement, will you promise to at least consider that women should be able to vote?"

He bowed over her hand. "If those are the terms, then yes. I can agree to try and be more open-minded."

Silence fell between them while she considered his offer.

At last, she spoke. "Then, fine. I'll agree to it. But the first time you rile me..."

"I know, I know. You'll sock me." He feigned receiving a blow, then covered his eye.

"Don't mock me, Gregory." Her words were sharp, but her beautiful face held a smile.

Behind him, the doors of the saloon swung open, and rowdy bunch of men entered. Their boisterous laughter and loud conversation quickly turned the quiet saloon into a noisy space. The men chose the largest table in the center of the space, the only one large enough for a group of the size.

He released her hand, and she eased away. "Get on home, Gregory. I've got customers and you're a distraction."

He drained the last of his drink. "What if I want to sit here and drink sarsaparilla all night?"

Her brow creased, she pointed toward the door. "You've

had your drink, and you got what you wanted. Now, git!"

Noting the mirth behind her words, he sat his Stetson on his head. Tipping it to her, he meandered out.

Outside, full dark had fallen. The pole mounted oil lamps lining the street illuminated his path as he moved down the plank walk toward the Taylor Hotel. He lived in a room on the third floor, which was set aside by the Taylor family for regular boarders. Noah often asked him why he didn't have a small cabin built for himself, but as a single man with no attachments, he didn't see any need. His life consisted of working for the people of Ridgeway, the occasional poker game or fishing expedition, and little else. For a man living the way he did, a small room was all he needed. With no grass to mow, animals to care for, or crops to plant, boarding at the Taylor Hotel suited him just fine. He opened the door, avoiding the fancy glass pane, and removed his hat as he stepped inside.

In the lobby, he nodded to the elder daughter Kelly Taylor, who was working the desk. On his way up the stairs, he passed young Marcus Taylor, carrying a stack of bathing sheets. No older than ten, Marcus helped his family in cleaning and stocking the rooms. He greeted the boy, then moved down the third floor corridor toward his room.

He was about to extract his key when he heard approaching footsteps. Turning, he smiled at Eugenia Taylor, moving toward him with a basket. She and her husband Milford, who'd moved to Ridgeway from Charlotte, North Carolina several years ago, owned the hotel.

"Evenin', Gregory." A thin smile brightened her otherwise stern countenance.

"Mrs. Taylor. How are you this evening?"

"Just fine, son. Need any fresh towels?" She gestured to the basket in her hands.

"Sure, I could use a few." He removed two clean towels from the pile and slung them over his shoulder. "Thanks."

"No problem. Oh, and one more thing."

"Yes?"

"I understand you're 'involved' with Angel May. Is that right?"

He inclined his head. "That only just happened today. How do you know about it?"

Eugenia's face crinkled, as if she were confused. "As I understood it, y'all were kissing in the saloon several days ago. Getting along like two hogs in slop, as I heard it." Her time living in California had only softened her Southern drawl by a small margin, and she still spoke with the colorful language of her home.

He drew a deep breath as he remembered the day he'd argued with Angel, only to have her kiss him. Ridgeway was a small town, and anyone walking by the saloon could have seen them. Still, he was curious about her source. "Mrs. Taylor, may I ask who told you that?"

"Mrs. Corcoran. She told all the ladies at the quilting circle. We all agree it's about time you settled down."

He closed his eyes briefly and stifled a groan. Angel's aunt had seen them; that fact had slipped his mind until now. Why she'd felt the need to inform an entire group of gossiping biddies about it, he couldn't guess. Whatever the case, his private business was probably now on the lips of every woman in town.

Eugenia continued chattering. "I don't mind it, myself. Not one bit. You're free to court her if you choose. She's a nice girl, a bit unconventional, but still nice. All I ask is that you remember hotel policy about *unmarried couples*." She crinkled her brow to emphasize the last two words.

"Yes, ma'am, I remember. Don't worry. I won't be bringing Miss Lane here." He'd been informed when he took the room that he couldn't bring ladies past the lobby, until such time as he took a wife. He didn't necessarily agree with the Taylors' overly moral stance, but it was their business to run as they saw fit.

"Good, I'm glad to hear it. Because you know me and

Milford don't run *that kind* of establishment. We may be out west but we still want to inject as much southern gentility into this place as we can."

He said nothing, knowing she was probably only pausing to take a breath, not to let him voice his opinion.

"Anyhow, like I said, I approve. If you're gonna be sheriff, it'll look much better if you have a wife. Good wife helps ground a man, you know. Gives him a sense of responsibility, makes him more thoughtful."

He blinked. *Did she just say, wife?* He'd been courting Angel May all of three hours, and the biddies of town were already planning the wedding.

"Well, have a good night, Gregory." She shifted the basket in her arms, then moved on down the corridor toward the large suite she shared with her husband and two children.

Unlocking the door with the key he kept in his vest pocket, he entered his room and closed the door behind him.

His room was as simple a space as his uncomplicated life allowed. It was of good size, and held a large poster bed, dresser, a dining table and chair, as well as a wardrobe, all built of sturdy pine. The hardwood floor was covered by a single, large woven burlap rug. An armchair occupied a corner of the room, between the bed and the window, and that was where he often sat to read the morning paper, if he didn't have early duty.

He hung his vest inside the wardrobe, placing his Stetson on the flat top with its kin. As he gathered his soap and shaving things in preparation for a trip to the bathing room, he thought about what Eugenia had said. Out of all her idle chatter, one phrase had stood out to him.

"If you're gonna be sheriff, it'll look much better if you have a wife."

He hadn't given much thought to it, but he supposed she was right. He'd heard Noah talk about the way folks seemed more willing to obey his edicts, and were generally easier to deal with, since he'd married Miss Valerie. Maybe there was some benefit to having a wife on his arm. If nothing else, it would get the biddies to cease their hypothesizing about when he might "settle down".

He thought of his older brother Jack, and the way he'd mellowed since marrying his wife. As a boy, Jack had been as rough and tumble as they came, and now that he'd married, he did things he'd never done before like reading and attending plays. Despite the changes, Jack seemed very content with his new life.

With his shaving things in the bag, he opened his door and poked his head out, to see if the chatty Eugenia might be in the hall again.

Once he'd determined it was safe, he eased out and headed for the bathing room.

Chapter 5

Her protest sign tucked beneath her arm, Angel opened the door to Lilly's Dress Emporium and stepped inside.

Within the confines of the dress shop, several of the women of town were already gathered. This small but determined contingent of about twenty women was led by Prudence Emerson, wife of the town's reverend, and the librarian Prissy Parker. They'd dubbed themselves the Crusaders for the Vote.

The ladies all stood in various spots among the racks displaying Lilly Beningno's latest creations, conversing amongst themselves. As Angel moved further inside, she shared greetings with them. Some smiled and responded in kind, while others cut her a censuring look. Unsure of what could be causing their sour attitudes, she found an empty spot near the counter and moved into it to wait for the meeting to begin.

Soon, Prissy stepped up on a crate behind the sales counter. She wore her typical librarian's garb of a dark skirt and white shirtwaist with a crocheted collar. Raising her hand, she called the meeting to order. "Good Morning, ladies. Thanks for coming today. We've got a very unique protest planned that's sure to get the men's attention."

The tall, graceful Prudence, dressed in a simple yellow day dress, nodded her head in agreement. "Yes. Today, they won't be able to ignore us. We're going to hit them right where it smarts."

Lilly raised her hand. "We ought to. Did you all see the article in the Tribune the other day? About how the deputy doesn't want us voting? Why, he's about as bad as that spiteful reporter at the San Francisco Chronicle."

Being reminded of the article made Angel's face wrinkle into a frown. Not only had Gregory made those remarks, but the reporter McCormack had also included remarks from several men of town, some of who had been listed only as 'a male citizen.' They'd spouted pretty much the same sexist views. Even though the article attemp6ted to paint an objective portrayal of the opposing views folks had on the suffrage issue, it had still raised her ire.

Prissy said, "I saw it. That's why we're going to fix them, and fix them good."

Angel couldn't help but smile as the women chattered around her. The air held a sense of excitement, because they all knew Prudence was right. They'd come up with a truly clever way to cause a noticeable, yet harmless disruption. Aside from that, she wouldn't have to break the vow she'd made to Gregory the day he'd arrested her. What they had planned today wouldn't affect traffic in any way, at least not on the roads.

Prissy's voice rang out over the assembly again. "Now, we all know our places, correct? Because once we get there, there won't be any time for dilly dallying."

Everyone responded affirmatively. They'd gone over their plan several times over the last few days, so by now they all knew their assignments.

"Good. There's one more matter we ought to address before we leave."

Angel looked around, wondering what Prissy might want to discuss. To her surprise and confusion, most of the women in the room seemed to be looking directly at her.

Not one to shrink from a challenge, Angel called, "What is everyone staring at?"

Prissy clicked her teeth. "We all know about you and the deputy, Angel May."

She groaned. So her personal life was now grist for the gossip mill. She and Gregory hadn't even been out on their first courting excursion, and already folks were talking about them. "So? What of it?"

Prissy faltered. "It's none of our concern, really. We just..."

"Don't cotton to your consorting with the enemy." Eugenia finished Prissy's sentence.

Angel rolled her eyes. "Look here, all of you. Yes, I'm courting Gregory. And Prissy's right, it's not any of your concern. He isn't going to change my way of thinking. I'm just as committed to us getting the vote as always."

Prudence intervened before anyone else could make a smart remark. "That's good enough for me. Now let's get our wits about us, and get ready to go. It's nearly eleven thirty."

Angel took a deep breath to calm her nerves. How could these women, many of whom she considered friends, interrogate her like that? As the women began to form a line by the door in preparation for the march, Angel strode over to the librarian, who was climbing down from the crate she'd been standing atop.

As soon as Prissy was on solid footing, Angel got hold of her arm. "Prissy, what's the matter with you? Why would you even bring that up?"

Prissy looked a bit chastised. "There was concern from some of the ladies. I didn't want to make a fuss, I swear."

"What ladies?"

Prissy directed her eyes at the ground. "I won't name them, but mainly the older women."

Angel released her grip on Prissy's arm. "Fine. But I'd appreciate it if you didn't subject me to any more questioning, just to satisfy the nosy biddies among us."

Prissy gave a half-smile. "I won't. Sorry about that, Angel."

Angel gave Prissy a playful tap against the forehead. She knew Prissy's heart was in the right place. The librarian much preferred being in charge of books over being in charge of people, and was probably just trying to keep the peace.

With that bit of unpleasantness settled, Angel took her place in the line of women holding signs. With so many of them in Lilly's shop at once, the line stretched across the sales floor all the way back to the back room where Lilly did her sewing and stored her fabrics and notions.

As for the shop owner, she stood just outside, propping open the door. From her vantage point, Lilly was watching the big clock that had recently been installed on the third floor facade of the Taylor Hotel. "Alright, ladies. It's eleven thirty."

Prissy, at the back of the line, called out, "Let's go, Crusaders!"

The line of women began to move quickly and quietly out the open door of the shop and onto the walk bordering Town Road. Some carried signs or placards, but no one chanted or spoke- at least not yet. They were saving that for their destination.

As Angel and Prissy left the shop, bringing up the rear of the line, Lilly locked the door and fell in behind them.

Angel drew her short cape tighter against the slight chill in the air, and kept her eyes focused on the women moving ahead of her. As was typical of this time of day, there were a few people out on the walks, going about their daily business. Those in the path of the column of silent women stepped aside to allow them to pass, while watching with curious eyes.

As they filed past the hat shop next to Lilly's, the milliner Zelda Graves stepped out. Her "Closed" sign was hung on the door, and Zelda took her place in line behind Lilly.

Angel knew they made quite a sight, the long line of women marching up the walk in such a sizable group. Today, there would be no circling about in the streets, no holding up traffic; yet they knew what they were planning would have an impact. They moved as a unit, the picture of quiet determination, with a singular goal in mind. They wanted change, and they aimed to get it.

She remembered her days as a young girl, hearing of her aunt's travels. She and her mother had Lucille led a relatively quiet life on the edge of town, a life that might have been boring without Myrna. She always returned from her theater company tours with wonderful stories of gracing stages in exciting locales and meeting all sorts of interesting people. Myrna had even participated in suffrage marches in New York, during performance tours of the area. Angel liked to think of herself as a product of the influence of the two women who'd raised her. She had Lucille's kindness of spirit, and her aunt Myrna's sense of adventure. What greater adventure could there be than to be a catalyst for change; to have an affect on the lives of women who weren't even born yet?

Angel felt the smile spreading across her face as the women crossed Town Road. It would only be a few minutes before they reached their destination, and when they did, the men of town would have no choice but to listen.

***

Gregory thumbed through the reports he'd been filling out for the last hour, checking them over one last time. His stomach rumbled again, this time loudly enough for Thaddeus Stern, his shift-mate, to hear it.

The light horseman chuckled from his seat at the small table by the door, across from where Gregory sat at the big desk. "Deputy, I think it's time you went for lunch."

Shaking his head, Gregory stamped the top of the stack and tucked the papers into the desk drawer. "I thing you're right, Thad. Do you want me to bring you back something?"

The younger man shook his head, barely looking up from his own weekly patrol reports. "I went by Ruby's this morning and picked up a sack lunch to go. I'm fine."

"Alright then. I should be back within an hour." Gregory stood, shrugged his duster on over his shirt, vest, and denims. This morning had been uncharacteristically chilly, and he thought he might need the coat again to stave of any remaining chill. Plucking his black Stetson from hat rack, he placed it atop his head and strode out into the afternoon sunshine.

The big clock on the Taylor hotel showed the hour to be about a quarter past noon. He crossed the street at the intersection when vehicle traffic allowed, moving north along the plank walk bordering Town Road.

When he came to Ruby's, Ridgeway's only restaurant and the last business on the northernmost border of town, he saw a gaggle of folks standing outside. While a crowd was pretty typical of lunchtime at Ruby's, he couldn't recall ever seeing this many men waiting outside. Aside from that, they weren't in an orderly line. Instead, they were all lined up along the front of the building, like children peering in the windows of a candy store.

Gregory moved closer to see what all the commotion was about, and as he did, he picked up on the faint sound of female voices. *Are they singing?* If they were, he couldn't guess why; this was hardly the time and place for a choir rehearsal.

He tapped the shoulder of a man leaning against the door of the place. The man turned around, and he saw that it was young Levell Davis, who sometimes worked at Buck's Barbershop as an apprentice.

"Levell, what's going on in there?"

Levell spoke hurriedly as he relayed what he knew. "It's the womenfolk. They been in there the whole lunch hour so far, singing and chanting. There ain't a seat to be had!"

The young man stepped back and allowed Gregory to see for himself. As he looked inside through the glass pane at the top of the restaurant door, he could see the women, doing just as Levell had said. They occupied every stool at the lunch counter, and every seat at every table in the place. At the moment, they were chanting loudly, "We Hunger for the Vote!" Among them was Angel May, who was seated atop the lunch counter. Her denim clad legs were crossed demurely, but her manner was boisterous as she hoisted a sign that read "Let Us Vote" over her head.

The few men who'd made it inside were standing in the middle of the female contingent, all of them vying to get near the lunch counter. A few of them were leaning against the door as they waited, which prevented anyone else from entering.

He stepped back from the door and pressed his hand to his forehead. Of all the trouble making, disruptive, fool-headed things to do. The men in Ridgeway and the surrounding towns worked hard, toiling all day to feed their families. The last thing they needed was this gaggle of crazy females keeping them from getting a decent meal.

His stomach growled again, and he made up his mind. Pushing his hat forward on his head, he squared his shoulders. "Alright, stand back. I"m going in there."

Those gathered outside back away, and Gregory pounded on the door. The men inside turned around, and seeing the deputy sheriff there, stepped aside. Gregory swung the door open and entered, his eyes focused squarely on Angel May.

He raised his hand and his voice, shouted over the din. "Enough!"

The chanting ceased, and the women put lowered their signs and placards. All eyes fell on him.

Satisfied that he had their attention, he kept his gaze on Angel as he spoke. "Now see here. I realize you women think you've got a cause to defend. But these men have been working hard and they deserve to get a meal. Kindly clear outta here now, or I'll haul you all in for disturbing the peace!"

The men in the room cheered, but the women groaned.

Ever the firecracker, Angel May piped up. "You can't do that. The jail won't hold all of us." Her eyes flashed with the challenge.

In response, the ladies cheered and applauded.

He held up his hand again. "Stifle, all of you!" Then he addressed Angel. "It's true the jail won't hold all of you, Miss Lane. But it'll hold you just fine."

Her eyes widened. "You wouldn't haul me in again!"

In response to her statement, he strode across the room to where she sat on the counter. "I can, and I will." He took the bracelets from his belt loop, and while her eyes shot daggers at him, he secured her wrists.

"I'm not going back to jail, Deputy." She turned up her nose, made a show of ignoring him.

Gregory noticed how quiet the restaurant's interior had grown. Since he knew everyone was gossiping about him and Angel May courting, he decided to use this opportunity to let them all know she'd get no special treatment.

So, with everyone present watching, he grasped her at the waist, lifting her off the counter.

She uttered an outraged shout. "Put me down, you jackass!"

"Gladly. But you will be coming with me to the jail. Put up anymore fuss, and I'll carry you there, and add a second charge for resisting arrest."

She made a sound of disgust. "Fine. Just set me down before I sock you and get a third charge."

He set her feet on the floor, and eased up to the counter with one hand on the chain between the cuffs.

Ruby, the proprietor, stood there with her jaw hanging open.

Addressing her, Gregory said, "Could you wrap me up a ham sandwich and an order of Saratoga chips, please? I'll take it with me."

Still staring, Ruby nodded. "Sure thing, Deputy."

He called out behind him, "Form a line behind me for your orders. And ladies, make yourselves scarce before I round you up."

All present did as he asked. The men started to form an orderly line behind him. The women grumbled as they left their positions and filed out, freeing up the tables and stools.

While he waited for his food, he hazarded a glance at his

angry prisoner. She swiveled her head, refusing to make eye contact with him. Her lips were pursed tighter than the lid on a mason jar. Parts of him wanted to chuckle at her pouting, but he held himself in check.

When Ruby handed him the small canvas sack containing his lunch, he turned and gave the chain a tug. "Alright. Let's go."

"Hmph." Still refusing to look at him, she followed him out of the restaurant. They moved in tandem down the street and back across to the sheriff's office.

Inside, Thad jumped up from his seat. Seeing the sour faced Angel, he asked, "Could you use a hand, Deputy?"

Gregory nodded. "Open up the first cell so Miss Lane can cool her heels."

Thad grabbed the keys from the wall behind his table, and did as he was asked. Gregory escorted his angry companion into the cell, freed her wrists, and then stood back as Thad locked her in.

The young light horseman replaced the keys on the nail in the wall. Thad looked between Angel's angry face, and Gregory's indifferent one. Then, he asked, "Would now be a good time for my coffee break?"

Gregory chuckled, knowing Thad had picked up on the tension between he and Angel. "Go on, Thad. Be back in quarter of an hour."

Once Thad strolled out, Gregory sat down at his desk, set on finally feeding his growling stomach. He removed the sandwich from the bag, unwrapped the linen surrounding it, and took a bite. As always, Ruby's ham was tender and well seasoned, and nestled between two thick slices of her her heavenly, butter-laden bread.

From inside the cell, Angel cleared her throat.

His seat behind the big desk allowed him to see directly into her cell, which was to his left. Only a strip of flooring about six feet wide separated the desk from the cell block.

When he'd swallowed the bite of food, and washed it down

with some water from the canteen he kept at the desk, he turned her way. "Something you need, Miss Lane?"

She released a bitter laugh. "Sure, Deputy. What I need is to know why I was fool enough to say I'd court you."

He shrugged as he chewed another bite of the sandwich. "Don't know. Had you had much to drink that day?"

She looked at him, her eyes narrowed. "Oh, is this amusing to you, Gregory? You find this funny?"

"A bit."

"If I weren't locked in here, I'd wallop you good."

"Then I'd just have to call the sheriff in, and have you hauled off to Oakland to see the marshal."

She harrumphed, folded her arms over her chest. "You're such an ass."

He looked at her sitting there, with the fabric of the tight denims clinging to her shapely hips, and the frilly red blouse she wore revealing the graceful curve of neck and collarbone. Even wearing that sour puss, she was a beauty. "I know you're angry with me. But I have a job to do, you know."

"There was no reason to arrest me again. You didn't give me time to..."

"Time to what? Talk my ear off about how women ought to have the vote? I've had my fill of that, thanks."

She sat back against the wall and lapsed into angry silence.

He raked his gaze over the lines of her face, so tense with frustration. She believed in her cause, he had to give her that much. Though she was currently a prisoner, that fact didn't stop him from wanting to rake his hands through the dark riches of her hair, and kiss her pouting lips until her anger melted like sugar in a steaming cup of coffee.

"You're beautiful when you're angry, Angel."

She rolled her eyes his way. "I'm not speaking to you, Gregory Simmons."

"Ah, but you just did, my dear." He got up from the desk, sidled over to the cell.

Their eyes connected.

He winked at her.

She gave him an exaggerated roll of her eyes.

Nonplussed, he waited, watching her.

A hint of a smile crossed her face.

"Is that a smile I see?" He teased her, his hands gripping the bars.

"Gregory..." her tone chastised him, yet still held a hint of humor.

"Maybe I can win your heart yet." He winked at her again.

The reddish color rising in her cheeks, along with the way she covered her mouth to hide her smile, gave away that her mood had lightened somewhat.

"I'm not going to ask for bail this time. Your friends can keep their money."

She seemed relieved to hear him say that. Uncovering her mouth, she said in a wry tone, "Your mercy knows no bounds, warden."

He chuckled. "Just be glad of it, Angel."

Their gazes connected again. She lowered her eyes, batting the long, dark fringe of her lashes in the most appealing way. The gesture reminded him of why he'd asked her to court him. She was a firecracker on the outside, but inside her there was a soft, feminine treasure, one he hoped to reveal.

He was so caught up looking at her that he didn't notice Thad returning from his break. When the young man cleared his throat, he turned to see him standing in the doorway, grinning.

Gregory furrowed his brow. "What's so funny, Thad?"

"So it's true. You and Miss Lane are..."

Gregory shook his head as he finished the statement. "Yes. Angel and I are courting. Since when do lawmen participate in idle gossip?"

Thad only grinned wider as he retook his seat behind the small table. "It's all over town, Deputy. In a place like

Ridgeway, gossip is near impossible to avoid."

He knew Thad was right.

When he glanced back at Angel, she raised her hand to her lips and blew him a kiss. "Any chance of a prisoner getting an early release for good behavior?"

Shaking his head, he went for the keys.

Chapter 6

Letting herself in the back door of her apartment, Angel slipped inside and closed the door behind her. It was nearing the dinner hour, and she dearly hoped her aunt was out, perhaps with the ladies of her quilting circle, or the bible study group she often attended.

She took slow, quiet steps over the braided rug toward her bedroom. She heard no sign of her aunt's presence, only the muffled sound of a few conversations coming from the saloon up front.

She placed her hand on the knob of her bedroom door.

"Angel May, you may as well quit sneaking around and face me, Missy."

Angel sighed, her shoulders slumping as she turned toward her aunt's voice. "Aunt Myrna, I thought you'd be out."

Myrna emerged from behind the bamboo screen that separated her sleeping area from the parlor, with a look of censure on her aged face. "Nonsense. It's Thursday evening and I have no place to be but home. Now what's this I hear about you being arrested again?"

Her shoulders slumped, and she hung her head. "I was protesting with the Crusaders, and Gregory decided to abuse his authority and haul me in for disturbing the peace."

Myrna folded her thin arms over her chest, rustling the fabric of the voluminous silk kimono she wore. She'd brought the garment back from a tour of the Orient. "That's not what I heard, Angel. Eugenia says you goaded him."

Angel rolled her eyes. *Eugenia Taylor's lips never cease their flapping.* "Well, I may have, but only a little."

Myrna wagged an aged finger in her direction. "Angel, you're tempting fate. You know that if you're arrested three times on the same charge, the town charter says you're to go before the marshal in Oakland. Is that what you want to do?"

"No, but I..."

Her aunt cut her off. "Then for goodness sakes, stop provoking the man. Find another way to bring him around to our way of thinking. You two are courting, aren't you?"

She nodded, knowing there was no sense in denying it. She and Gregory were apparently the talk of the town. Even some of the other Crusaders had made their interest known, by way of the not-so-subtle questions they'd peppered her with.

By now, her aunt had moved into the parlor area, and was making herself comfortable on the settee. "Then I suggest you use your feminine talents to persuade him, because I don't want to see you get into any more trouble."

She took a seat next to her aunt, looked into the dark eyes of the woman who'd helped her mother raise her. Surely she wasn't saying..."Aunt Myrna!"

She waved her off. "Don't look so shocked, girl. I've traveled much of the world, and America isn't the only place where a woman's expected to go her whole life in docile servitude and unquestionable virtue."

Having never traveled outside the country, Angel had never given much thought to what women's lives were like in other countries. She'd been too busy trying to improve things in her own life. "What do you mean?"

"Many cultures of the world are male dominated, just like ours. Those women suffer under much the same chauvinism as we do. But there are places in Africa where societies are matrilineal, and the women hold all the power."

Angel thought such a society sounded very progressive. "I doubt that will happen here."

"So do I. But we can still work toward something better than what we have. That's where your feminine wiles come in, honey. Use what you've got to get what you want."

"Mama would be so scandalized to hear you say that." A smile touched her lips at the memory of her sweet, soft-spoken mother.

Myrna laughed. "I bet she would. My sister was as straight-laced as they come."

A silent moment passed between them, and Angel's mind replayed some of the happy times she'd had with her mother. Looking at her aunt, she sensed Myrna was doing the same.

Finally Myrna spoke again. "Anyhow, I never had any children, but I love you like you were my own. Promised Lucy I would take care of you. So, I'm not advising you to be loose or immoral. You can move a man plenty without lifting your skirts. Remember that, alright?" She gave her Angel's thigh a few soft pats with her open palm.

Angel nodded her head, internalizing the advice. Myrna Lane Corcoran had never been anyone's shrinking violet, having left home as a teenager to travel with an acting troupe. As a child, Angel had waited impatiently for her aunt to return from her tours, anticipating the bounty of stories and souvenirs Myrna would bring home. In those days, her aunt never disappointed her. She'd always looked up to her worldly, well-traveled aunt, and even now, she continued to do so.

This was advice Myrna had given her before. She'd married young, to a fellow actor named Russell Corcoran. They'd traveled together for fifteen years, until his untimely death when he fell headfirst from a stage during a performance. All of this had occurred before Angel's birth, but she was familiar with the story. Though she was thirty three years old, nearly thirty years younger than her aunt, they'd enjoyed something like a sisterly camaraderie. Myrna had loved Russell dearly, and still spoke of him affectionately decades after his death.

As an widow, Myrna knew society expected her to either

mourn then remarry, or spend the rest of her life in mourning and without the company of another man. But with no desire to enter another marriage, and even less desire to go to her grave without ever experiencing a man's affections again, Myrna had chosen her own path. She entertained the gentlemen she deemed worthy, and did so discreetly, keeping her dignity intact.

Myrna's voice broke into her thoughts. "Remember, Angel. Your body is your own, despite what society may say. Who you choose to share it with is your own business. You're a good girl, I know you'll handle things the right way."

Needing some time to process her aunt's words before she started the evening shift in the saloon, Angel excused herself and went to her bedroom.

The space was as simple as the woman who occupied it. White lace curtains hung at the lone window, which faced the green forests bordering the northwestern end of town. The poster bed was dressed with plain white sheets and a pink and white quilt she'd made as girl. The dresser holding her clothes was also home to a few bottles of perfume, some hair ornaments, and her grooming supplies. The short legged oak table beside her bed held a gas lamp, and a small framed portrait of her mother, Lucille.

Aunt Myrna was the antithesis of her younger sister. Lucille had been a schoolteacher, as well as a quiet spirit and pious parishioner of the old church headed by the late Reverend Thomas Earl. When she wasn't at the schoolhouse, or at the church, Lucille had spent her time lovingly attending to Angel's needs, and teaching her the skills a proper woman of society should have. In her youth Angel had learned to cook, clean, sew, and read music, all at her mother's knee. Aunt Myrna had taught her how to make pottery, apply face paints and style her hair, as well as how to protect herself. The three of them had been an unconventional family, yet Angel didn't feel anything she'd lacked anything in her raising.

Angel knew nothing about her father; all she knew was that her mother had never been married to him. Some of the folks in town had been cruel to her and her mother due to that, but she'd been taught to ignore the slurs hurled at her. The older she got, the less attention she paid to the harpies in town. Finally they stopped bothering her. She assumed they lost interest in teasing her, once they realized they wouldn't get a rise out of her.

She sat down on the edge of the bed and took a deep breath. Her courtship with Gregory was still less than a week old, and she knew that if she followed her aunt's advice, things would get much more serious between them. She wasn't a prude by any stretch, as she'd entertained her share of young men. While she wasn't one who shared her body indiscriminately, she knew that things were bound to progress to the carnal realm if she engaged Gregory with her "wiles."

What would it mean to share herself with Gregory? It would not be all about "persuading" him, as aunt Myrna had suggested. The physical attraction between them was real, and palpable. She knew that if she opened that door, and let their relationship go to a physical level, there was a good chance there would be no going back.

She went to her wardrobe, pulled out her the apron she sometimes wore over her clothes when working in the saloon. In less than an hour, her shift would start. The Thursday night crowd could get pretty thick, so she needed to focus on taking care of her customers. With that in mind, she tied the apron strings behind her, fixed her hair into a bun, and left the room, headed for the saloon up front.

Her aunt, still on the settee, winked as she passed. "Think about what I said, Angel. Sometimes it's the only way to get a man to thinking clearly."

She nodded, but said nothing as she slipped form the apartment, closing the door behind her.

***

Kianna Alexander

Sidestepping past the many chairs set up in rows in the lobby of the Taylor Hotel, Gregory found a seat near the back, and sat. It was a clear, warm Friday night, and most of the folks in town were present for the final debate between the two mayoral candidates. With the hotel being the largest structure in town, the lobby often served as the location for town gatherings such as this. There was talk of building a town hall, as well as a theater for the performing arts, but Gregory didn't think too much of the rumors. To his mind, the matter of such things would be left up to whoever won the election.

All around him, citizens of Ridgeway were present. Most were seated, but a few stood about in the corners of the room, carrying on muted conversations. The hotel staff had propped opened the big double doors that separated the lobby from the dining room to create a larger space. The expanded space had been set with as many rows of chairs as could be fit while still allowing a center aisle for walking, and a space up front, near the check-in desk, where two podiums had been set up for the candidates.

As he waited for the event to begin, he looked around the nicely appointed room. The Taylors had opened the hotel back in '83, after more than a year of construction. The fancy striped wallpaper and soft imported carpets gave the place an air of sophistication. Several large prints by Currier and Ives hung from the walls, as did sconces that held gas lamps. During one of his many chats with Eugenia Taylor, she'd spoken of the family's plans to upgrade to electric lighting before the end of the decade. As a tenant there, he was pleased with their progressive attitude. The upgrades they made would only serve to make his life easier and more convenient.

On the right side of the room, across the aisle from where he sat, Gregory saw the gaggle of women, seated in the three rows closest to the front. They were the same sign toting, chanting troublemakers that had been causing all the interruptions to town life as of late. For the moment, at least, they seemed content to converse among themselves, and as far as he could tell no one had a sign or placard. He hoped they'd behave themselves during the debate, but decided to keep an eye on them, just in case.

He didn't see Angel among the women, but he knew she wouldn't miss the debate. He sat, minding his own affairs, but let his eyes dart to the door whenever someone entered.

When Angel appeared, he watched intently as she strolled down the center aisle. When he saw what she was wearing, his jaw dropped. She'd donned a skirt and a blue shirtwaist with lace edging the collar and the wrists of the long sleeves. Having not seen her in a dress or skirt since the town Christmas social nearly two years prior, he was shocked to see her dressed that way.

As she breezed past, she looked his way. The dark eyes held a sultry invitation as she inclined her head toward him. A small smile lifted the corners of her pink painted lips, but she said nothing.

She held his eyes for a moment.

He detected something very seductive in her gaze. It quickened his pulse and heated his blood, sending it rushing for the lower regions of his body.

She dropped her gaze, freeing him from her spell. Then she moved on to join the women seated up front.

When she took her seat, he found himself still gazing at her, though he was now looking at her back and the glossy riches of her dark hair, bound up in a fashionable chignon. Something had passed between them just now, and he couldn't wait for this debate to end. When it did, he meant to take her someplace private, so he could experience the full heat of the fire he'd seen behind her eyes.

Bernard Ridgeway's booming voice called the gathering to order, and Gregory turned toward the front. Bernard made

Kianna Alexander

a few statements about the order of things before stepping away.

Noah and his opponent, Nathan Greer, came together briefly for a handshake, then took their places behind the podiums.

On the front row sat Kyle McCormack, the reporter for the Ridgeway Tribune, who was to act as moderator. McCormack stood to shake hands with each man, then launched into his first question.

"Gentleman, tariff policy is an issue of utmost importance, both locally and on the national level. What is your position on the tariff? Mr. Greer, you may go first."

Nathan Greer, a burly man with close trimmed brown hair and a full mustache, grasped the lapels of his suit as he spoke. "I believe the tariff should be lowered. Business owners and shippers should not have to bear the expense of these prohibitive fees."

McCormack nodded. "And Sheriff Rogers, your views?"

Noah laced his fingers together atop the surface of the podium. "As with most topics, I disagree with Mr. Greer. Tariffs should be higher, for the simple reason that it's much fairer for those in business to bear the extra cost of producing and shipping goods. Everyday citizens are facing more than enough financial burden as it is."

Gregory half-listened as McCormack posed a question about pensions for veterans of the War Between the States, but his eyes were on Angel. Sitting there among the other ladies, hands in her lap, she seemed to be carefully following the debate. At the moment, she appeared to be just as demure and docile as any of her companions, yet he knew better. She was as feisty as they came, and her demeanor had turned out to be both vexing and tempting.

As if aware of his attention, she turned her head and looked right at him. Again, the dark eyes beckoned to him with an irresistible heat. A sultry smile crossed her face momentarily, then she refocused her attention on the debate. Straightening in his chair, he attempted to do the same.

McCormack took a sip of water from a tumbler sitting near him. " You've stated your positions on suffrage for women before, but I'd like to give you both an opportunity to clarify your positions. Sheriff, you may go first this time."

"Thank you. Folks, I see no good reason why our female citizens should be denied the vote. Now, I'm sure some of you will claim women are too addled or weak-minded. I know plenty of intelligent women, right here in our own town, who are plenty smart, smarter than some men if we're honest. I don't think anything negative can come from more people gaining a basic American right."

The women in the room gave Noah an enthusiastic ovation, while a few of the men booed and hissed. Gregory didn't express his opinion out loud, seeing no need to displease Angel now.

Nathan, his chest puffed up as if he were offended, took his turn next. "My opponent says women are fully capable of voting. I'm not so sure about that. But what I am sure of is that female capabilities are best put to use in the home. Their true calling is to serve their husbands, keep a clean home, and rear well-behaved children. Only through those God-given duties will they ever obtain any measure of happiness."

This time the men clapped. The women, for their part, stood and made a show of turning their backs on Greer. A few of them gathered their belongings and left, visibly upset.

Nathan seized on that. "You see? Women are much too temperamental and volatile. They aren't fit to be given the power of the ballot."

At that, Angel spun around to face the candidate. Her eyes were flashing with an angry fire. "Mr. Greer, what's between your ears ain't worth a heap of cow dung. If anybody in this room is unfit, it's you!"

The room erupted into bedlam. Angry shouts flew back and forth between the folks assembled. They all seemed to want to convince each other to change sides. With all the yelling and carrying on, that wasn't going to happen.

Gregory slid to the edge of his seat, watching the madness unfold. He kept his hand on his sidearm in case things came to blows.

A sharp series of raps from Bernard's gavel broke through the chaos. "Enough!" The old mayor's voice cut through any remaining chatter, and silence fell over the gathering.

His brow furrowed over his stormy eyes, Bernard rumbled again. "This is a debate, not a cockfight! We're all adults here, and will behave ourselves as such. Any more of this, and I'll have the lawmen toss you in the jail! Is that understood?"

Folks all around the room quieted.

Satisfied, Bernard nodded to McCormack.

McCormack straightened his tie, and continued on with things as if the fracas had never occurred. "So, Sheriff, you have two minutes to rebut Mr. Greer's last statement about why women should not be allowed the vote."

"Here's my rebuttal: If I'm elected, the women of this town cast their ballots in our next local election."

The remaining women, and a few like minded men, stood again and cheered for Noah, giving him his second ovation of the night. Watching Nathan Greer's tight face and squared shoulders, Gregory could tell Greer was more than a bit annoyed that his opponent was getting so many accolades from the audience.

McCormack waited for the applause to quiet. "Mr. Greer, am I to assume you would not extend such a right our female citizens, if you are elected?"

"You're damn straight I won't. And the sheriff should be ashamed of himself for pandering to these troublesome women!" Greer, with his chest puffed up like an angry grizzly, stepped away from his podium, then stomped down the center aisle and out the doors.

McCormack grinned. "I suppose that concludes our debate, then."

As the assemblage began to break up, Gregory rose and sought out Angel. Now that this formality was over, he wanted nothing more than to slip away to a private place with her.

He found her standing amongst a tangle of women, chatting. Minding his manners, he acknowledged her companions, the librarian Miss Parker and the schoolteacher Miss Smart. Then he waited as patiently as he could manage, his eyes on Angel the whole time.

Once the women said their goodbyes and parted, he reached out and captured Angel's soft hand within his own. "You look lovely this evening, my dear."

Her sultry eyes took on a coy look that made his pulse quicken. "I'm glad you approve, Gregory."

He eased her toward the door. "Come on. Let's go somewhere a bit more private, shall we?"

She let him guide her. "And just where would that be?"

He only smiled. "You'll see."

Kianna Alexander

Chapter 7

Angel held Gregory's hand and walked with him out of the hotel. He led her across the road to the library, and they went inside.

Only a few people were in the library this time of day, and it was due to close in less than an hour. Angel surmised that he'd brought her here for quiet, and there wasn't a much quieter place in town.

Prissy, seated behind her desk, looked up from an open book as they entered. As slight smile lifted the corners of her mouth, and she acknowledged their presence with a short nod before returning to her attention to her reading.

They moved to the small alcove by the front window that contained four upholstered armchairs. He took a seat, and she in sat the chair directly to his right.

She watched him removed his hat and place it on the small table centering the grouping of chairs.

He ran a hand through his dark locks. "I understand you enjoy reading. What kind of books do you like?"

She could feel her brow hitch with surprise. "How do you know I like to read?"

He shrugged. "The sheriff's office is right across the street from the library, and I've seen you coming in and going out with armloads of books. Your aunt has mentioned it to me, as well."

She felt some of her nervousness melt away, even as she wondered when he'd spoken to her aunt Myrna. He did frequent the saloon for his beloved sarsaparillas, and Myrna often played the upright piano near the bar, so it wasn't such a far-fetched idea. What really shocked her was that he cared enough to ask about her reading habits.

He eyed her expectantly. "So, are you going to tell me what sort of books you like?"

"Sure. I love fiction, mainly world literature and things written by authors from around the world. My aunt has introduced me to a lot of it."

He settled in to the chair. "Sounds like you have a broad taste. Tell me about some of your favorites."

She touched her chin, thinking on that for a moment. "I really enjoyed the 'One Thousand and One Nights,' it had a lot of wonderful and interesting stories. The only other one I've read that I liked was 'Treasure Island'. That's been my favorite book so far."

He fingertips moved along his chin in a slow, repetitive pattern. "Is that the book I've heard so much about, the one with the pirates?"

That made her smile. "Yes, it is a pirate story. Where did you hear of it?"

"A fellow was going on about it in the barber shop a few months back. He was a young man visiting on break from a university back east. He spent the entire morning telling everyone in the shop about it. Said it was the best book he'd ever read."

She tended to agree. "There was a lot of excitement in the book, I thought. It's about a pirate crew searching for an island that's said to be full of treasure, and all the adventures they have trying to find it. Folks go overboard, there's mutiny, fighting, and all sorts of other things going on in that book."

"I may have to read it one day while I'm on duty and nothing needs to be done. Who wrote it?"

"A Robert Louis Stevenson. He lives in Scotland, I believe. You know, he's also had a more recent book published that's also popular, 'The Strange Case of Dr. Jekyll and Mr. Hyde'. I haven't read that one yet, but it was published just about two years ago."

"And how long has Treasure Island been in print?"

She squinted a bit, trying to remember the date printed in her well worn copy of the tome. "I'm almost certain it came out back in '53."

He nodded. "Maybe I'll check out a copy of it, if they have it on hand. I don't read much but it does sound entertaining."

She giggled. "If the young man from the barber shop couldn't move you to read it, why would you bother now?"

"Something about the way you describe it makes me want to read it. If it can excite you, make your eyes light up this way, then I'd better see what it's all about."

Her cheeks warmed, and she cast her eyes downward. She'd never been one to play at being coy, but his words had touched her. She hadn't given any thought to it, but she supposed her demeanor had changed while she was describing her favorite book. She'd not had a conversation about literature with a man since Mr. Greenfield had retired and left her to run the saloon. He'd been the only other man she'd ever known who was both well read, and interested in discussing literature with her.

"There's something I wanted to ask you, Angel May."

His voice brought her back to the present, and she raised her gaze to meet his. "What is it?"

"I'd like to take you on a day trip, if that's acceptable."

Her interest piqued. She leaned over the arm of her chair, bringing her upper body closer to his. "Really? Where would we be going?"

"I have a very special destination in mind, but it's a surprise."

She thought on that for a moment. "If you won't tell me where we're going, how will I know how long the trip will take? And what sort of clothing should I wear?"

He released a deep, rumbling chuckle. "You're such a woman. Don't trouble yourself with the details, dear. Just let me handle everything."

She pursed her lips. "Come, now. You can't expect me to just run off with you to an unknown destination. I've a business to run, you know..."

He placed his big palm on her shoulder. The touch of his hand effectively cut off her complaint mid-sentence, as the warmth of his skin penetrated the thin fabric of her shirtwaist. He crooked the fingers of his other hand, and placed it beneath her chin.

Her mouth hanging aloft, she was forced to look directly into his penetrating gaze.

"Angel May, you may wear whatever you please. And the place I am taking you is within a day's journey. I'll pick you up just after breakfast, and return you home after the dinner hour. Does that suit you?"

She blinked once, then again. Looking into his eyes this way affected her ability to speak. He was so damned handsome her mind slowed, her thoughts were as scrambled as a basket full of baby chicks.

He repeated his question. "Does that suit you, sweetheart?"

The endearment make her cheeks feel even hotter. She wanted to say yes, tell him she'd go along to wherever it was he wanted to take her. But with midnight eyes focused so completely on her, she could only manage a feeble nod in response.

He smiled, as if pleased. "Good. I'm glad you agree. The trip will give me time to learn more about you."

She nodded again. He was still touching her, still looking at her.

Her lips tingled. Without thinking, she stuck her tongue out and swept it over them.

The quick gesture caught his eye. She saw his gaze dip a bit, knew he was watching her tongue travel over the surface of her lips.

He leaned his broad torso toward her, positioning his hands to cup her jawline gently. "God, you are lovely."

She sucked in a breath.

Before she could exhale again, he pressed his lips to hers.

The moment their mouths touched, she forgot the world

around them. Every cell in her body became enraptured with the warmth of his hands cupping her face, the firm pressure of his lips against hers, and the teasing of the tip of his tongue as he beckoned her to open to him.

She was powerless to deny him full access to her mouth, so she relaxed her jaw. He slipped his tongue between her lips, and it soon became entangled with her own. She gripped his strong, solid shoulders and held on. The arm of the chair pressed into her belly as she leaned in as close as she could get.

A sudden rapping sound echoed through the space.

She pulled away from him, and as she opened her eyes and looked around, she remembered where they were. Her cheeks heated again, this time from embarrassment, as she searched for the source of the sound.

Prissy was still seated behind her desk, but she had a small gavel in her hand. It was the gavel she usually banged when the interior of the library became too loud, but Angel knew the rapping had been for them. She mouthed a silent apology to her friend, who merely gave her a toothy grin in response.

Gregory chuckled. "I suppose we got a bit carried away."

She nodded, feeling sheepish. "We did. Thank heavens there are no children present."

They shared a bit of mutual laughter over their behavior. She knew the gossips would be volleying stories back and forth about them all over town, but she didn't care. She'd kissed him in public, and the deed couldn't be taken back. Frankly, she'd rather enjoyed kissing her beau, and what others thought of it was of little concern to her.

Giving voice to her thoughts, he said, "The gossip is only going to get worse, you know."

She shrugged. "I don't care. If they don't have anything better to do, let them talk about us."

"That's a good attitude to have."

She reached for his hand, clasped it with his. "So, when are we taking this trip?"

"I have my next day off day after tomorrow. Can you get away then?"

"Sure. The saloon's closed on Sundays, and whatever work I need to do can be put off."

"Good, then it's settled. I'd better walk you home."

She got to her feet, still holding his hand.

He stood and picked up his hat. "Let me see about the book, then we'll be on our way."

They stopped at the desk, and he inquired about a copy of Treasure Island.

Prissy rifled around in one of the crates of books she kept behind the desk. "I've got one here somewhere, that someone just turned in...ah, here it is." She extracted a copy of the book from beneath a few others, and handed it to Gregory.

He took it, and placed his signature in the ledger.

The librarian placed the pen back in the ink pot. "My pleasure. It will be due back on November 3, the day before the elections."

He placed his Stetson on his head and tucked the book beneath his arm. "Thank you, Miss Parker. After hearing Angel May talk about it, I just had to read it."

She smiled up at him, and he gave her an affectionate peck on the forehead.

Prissy tittered. "My, you two are really sparking."

For the third time this evening, Angel had to contend with the heat filling her cheeks. It seemed being around Gregory meant spending a lot of the time either blushing or overcome. Parts of her wondered what she'd really gotten herself into by agreeing to court him, but the woman in her reveled in his attentions, and looked forward to all they could share. Getting to know him certainly wouldn't be dull, that much she knew.

He asked, "Are you ready, Angel May?"

Already moving toward the door, she nodded. "It's

probably best, before Prissy takes a ruler to us."

He swiveled his head to look at her. "She can't do that. I'm the law."

She could only laugh as she shook our head. "If you think she won't, then you don't know our librarian very well."

He held the door open for her, and they stepped out into the damp evening air together.

***

Gregory was up before dawn on Sunday morning, getting ready for the day's excursion. As the light from the rising sun began to filter through the curtains of his room at the Taylor hotel, he stood before the small mirror hanging inside his wardrobe, straightening his tie. It had been years since he'd donned a suit as fine as this one to take a lady courting, and he knew he might be a bit rusty at this 'romance' thing. That wasn't going to stop him from doing his best to impress Angel May, and from getting to know as much about her as he could.

There was something about Angel May Lane that fascinated him, held him captive. What he knew of her now wasn't nearly enough to quench his curiosity. Today, they would spend two hours alone in a private coach he'd hired to take them to the Oakland Long Pier. He planned to spend the time in the coach conversing with her, touching her, and kissing her, away from the prying eyes of the nosy citizens of town. The idea of having her all to himself, even just for those two short hours, made a smile lift the corners of his mouth.

When they reached the pier, they would board a ferry carrying them across the bay to San Francisco. Once there, he had an afternoon planned that he hoped she would not soon forget. The city boasted many interesting sights and amusements to take in, but he'd chosen the one for them to visit that he thought she'd enjoy the most.

Satisfied with his appearance, he closed the wardrobe door. Gathering his hat and pocketing his wallet, he left his room and headed downstairs to the dining room.

It was just after seven, and the breakfast service was just beginning. When the hotel had first opened a few years ago, the dining room had only served pastries, tea, and coffee. Now the hotel's menu had been expanded to feature a light breakfast and dinner service, though it was still closed during the lunch hour. Most people in town brought a lunch with them to work; those that didn't visited Ruby's eatery.

He went directly to the buffet table, and made himself a plate. He then took his coffee and food to a table in the corner. As he ate the two biscuits filled with bacon and scrambled eggs, he took care not to soil his white shirt, or the jacket of his best black suit.

When he'd finished his breakfast, he moved to the counter. Kelly, the Taylor's daughter, saw him coming.

"Here you go, Deputy Simmons." She reached beneath the counter and hoisted a large basket up, handing it to him.

He thanked Kelly as he took the basket, containing the picnic meal he'd ordered for today's trip. With the handle of the basket firmly in his grasp, he placed his black Stetson atop his head and left the hotel.

A short stroll down the walk took him to the saloon, which was just next door. He leaned his back against the outer wall, by the swinging door, and waited as Angel has asked him to do the other night. Many of the folks who worked in town were already out on the walks and driving their vehicles down the road. A few of them cast curious glances in his direction. He merely tipped his hat to them. Yes, he was there to take Angel courting, but that wasn't any of their business. Their scrutiny reminded him of all the reasons he wanted to spirit her away from this place. Small town life could sometimes be stifling, and if they were truly going to make a go of this relationship, they'd need some

Kianna Alexander

privacy so they could get to know each other.

He heard her footsteps on the wooden floor inside the saloon before she opened the gate and stepped through the swinging doors and out onto the walk. He turned her way and offered a smile. "Good Morning, Angel May."

She returned his smile. "Good morning, Gregory. What's that you've got?" She gestured toward the large basket he carried.

He took a moment to let his eyes sweep over her. She'd chosen her usual clothing, a pair of denims that hugged her curves, along with a frilly yellow blouse. This one was cut a little differently than what he was used to, and covered her shoulders and collarbone. The pearl buttons were closed, right up to her throat. Her hair was pinned up at the crown of her head in some sort of chignon or bun. Whatever the style was called, it allowed him an unencumbered view of the smooth, angular lines of her face.

Her lips, painted a soft shade of red, parted again. "Gregory, did you hear me? What's in the basket?"

He snapped himself back to reality. "Sorry. You look so lovely today, I was distracted. Anyway, I have a picnic for us."

"Ah, another clue to today's mystery trip." She sucked on her bottom lip, her hazel eyes drifting upward as if she were thinking.

The gesture tantalized him. He knew she probably hadn't meant to tease him by suckling that lush lip, but that didn't stop his groin from tightening at the sight. He reached for her hand. "Let's go to the depot. Our coach will be here soon."

They waited a few moments for a lull in traffic, then crossed the road, hand in hand.

"Are we taking the stage to Oakland?"

He shook his head. "Not exactly. We are riding in a private coach."

Her eyes brightened with excitement as they stepped onto

the walk in front of the depot. "A private coach. My, I feel quite special."

"Good." He led her to a bench and gestured for her to sit.

Within a few minutes, the black coach, trimmed with gold and red paint and emblazoned with the words "Myers Coach Line" pulled up.

He stood, gave a gentle tug to the hand he still held. "Come, here's our coach now."

She followed him to the coach. By now, the coachman had left his seat, and was holding open the door. "Welcome aboard Myers Coach Line. Watch you step, miss."

She nodded to the man, then let Gregory help her inside. Once he joined her on the seat, the coachman closed the door behind them.

Shortly, the coach got underway.

Sitting next to her in the silent interior of the coach, Gregory placed his arm around Angel's shoulders. She eased a bit closer to him, until her denim clad hip rested against his own. He relished the feeling of holding her close to his side, with no one around to infringe on their privacy.

She scrutinized him, as if taking in his attire. "Are you sure I'm dressed right? I feel a bit under dressed, with you in your nice suit."

"No. I wanted to dress my best for you, but what you're wearing is just fine for where we're going."

She looked skeptical. "I don't know..."

He touched her satin cheek. "Don't worry. You look beautiful in whatever you wear, and you don't need formal attire where we're going. I promise."

She took on that coy expression, fluttering those thick dark lashes. "If you say so. Now that you've got me in the coach, are you going to tell me where we're going?"

He thought about it, and decided not to keep her wondering any longer. "Alright. I'm taking you to San Francisco."

She jumped, eyes wide. "Truly?"

"Yes. We're going to Golden Gate Park, to visit the Conservatory of Flowers."

"My, that sounds wonderful."

"I hope you'll enjoy it. Once we reach the pier in Oakland, we'll get the ferry across the bay."

She reached up, touched his jaw with graceful fingertips. "Thank you for this, Gregory. I've never been to San Francisco."

"Really? Not even once? It's not very far away."

She sighed. "I know. I've been close, just once. The liquor supplier I use for the saloon has their warehouse and offices outside the city limits, but I've never been to the city itself."

Knowing that he would be there to see her experience the vibrant city for the first time pleased him.

She gifted him with a soft kiss on the cheek. "I can't believe you're doing all this for me. The private coach, the ferry, the conservatory. It's really too much."

"Nothing could be too much for you, Angel May."

Her sparkling, tear damp eyes met his.

He knew at that moment that if they didn't start conversing, and soon, he would spend the entire coach ride kissing her, touching her, and possibly coaxing her right out of her clothes.

She removed a handkerchief from the pocket of her denims, dabbed her eyes. "What shall we do to pass the time?"

He could think of many things he'd like to do, none of which were appropriate while riding in a coach with a woman who was not his wife. "Let's talk. Tell me about your upbringing."

She leaned back against his arms, her gaze drifting up to the velvet lining of the coach's roof. "I grew up right outside of Ridgeway. My mother Lucille was a schoolteacher, and my aunt was an actress with a touring company. We went to the old Unity AME church..."

He listened intently, and noted that even though she was forthcoming about her childhood, she'd left something significant out. He watched her face as she spoke, wondering why she hadn't mentioned her father.

She paused, as if noticing his regard. "What is it?"

"I noticed you didn't mention a father."

Her expression changed, taking on a sadness he hadn't expected to see. "I never knew him. My mother knew his identity, but because they never married, she didn't like to speak of him. Whenever I asked, she simply told me it wasn't important."

He was a bit shocked to hear that. His own upbringing had been the opposite of hers. While she'd been reared by two women who loved her, he'd been surrounded by men. Other than his mother, all the people who influenced him as child had been male.

A silent moment passed as he wrestled with another question. He didn't want to cause her any more pain, but something compelled him to ask it. "Did you ever try to find him?"

Her face grew even more solemn as she replied. "My aunt helped me to search, after my mother's death. Aunt Myrna knew the name of the man my mother loved, so we went back to Houston, where mother and Myrna were born and raised. His name was Phineas Brock, and we did find him; in the local cemetery. He died during the Battle of Wilderness, fighting for the Rebs."

He took in her words, remembering how he'd felt hearing his own father read the newspaper coverage of that bloody battle. "I'm sorry, Angel May."

She shook her head. "It is what it is. Besides, Mr. Brock was married to another woman. That's why my mother never wanted to talk about him. She was ashamed."

Now that he knew a little more about Angel May, he found himself wanting to comfort her. So he wrapped her up in a protective embrace, and held her even closer.

She rested her head on his shoulder. "Now you know my story. What's your's?"

He blew out a breath. "Grew up on a farm outside of Sacramento. My folks grew vegetables, mainly avocados. It was me, my mother and father, two brothers, and my uncle and grandfather."

She whistled. "My, your mother had quite a passel to take care of."

He chuckled at that. "You're right. Just cooking us kept her in the kitchen most of the time. And the house was never clean for very long, because we boys were always roughhousing."

She was silent for a moment. "You told me before that your mother enjoyed taking care of your family, that she was fulfilled."

"Yes, I said that."

"You seemed so sure of it. Tell me, did you ever ask her?"

He furrowed his brow. "What do you mean?"

"I mean, did you ever ask her if she was happy taking care of such a large family? By your own accounts, you made a lot of work for her. My guess is you never inquired about her contentment, but you assumed she was happy, simply because she never raised her voice."

That observation gave him pause. Angel May had turned out to be very perceptive.

"Am I right?"

He groaned. "You're right. I never asked her."

"Then maybe you should rethink your views on how women ought to be spending their time. If you love your mother, and would make broad assumptions without asking her how she feels, then what of the rest of us?"

He felt his ire rising, but he tamped it down. Angel May was right. He'd never once asked his mother such a question, or even paused very long to consider it. He'd planned to spend the journey learning about his paramour, and instead, she was teaching him things about himself.

"I hope you're not cross with me, Gregory. I just had to speak my mind."

He gave her a gentle squeeze. "I'm not angry. Just surprised."

"I can be full of surprises, you know."

He heard the sultry invitation in her voice. "Show me, then."

She raised her face, pressing her lips against his.

Chapter 8

The morning's travels had left Angel a bit tired. But as she crossed the beautiful, verdant green grounds of San Francisco's Golden Gate Park with Gregory, she felt her energy return. The early afternoon sun warmed her skin. With every step, the soft green grass gave way like a plush carpet beneath her flat soled slippers. Alongside her, Gregory carried their picnic meal in one hand, his free hand cradling her own.

The stroll across the park was a long one, but she didn't mind it at all. Rather, she relished the experience. She couldn't recall every touring such a lovely place. The park's planning had obviously been well thought out. Golden Gate Park was to the bustling, progressive city of San Francisco what an oasis would be to a desert; an unspoiled place, set aside to allow people to leave their cares behind and enjoy the full bounty of nature. There were paths laid out for walking, to allow one to explore all the varieties of trees and plants set thriving on the grounds and observe the small animals scurrying about.

Gregory's voice cut through her musings. "What do you think of it so far?"

She sighed with contentment. "This place is absolutely beautiful."

"And we haven't even gotten to the Conservatory yet. You're going to love it."

"I don't doubt it."

As they drew closer to their destination, they passed by another building. It was one story, and she could see a lot of foot traffic going in and out of the building. As her gaze rose toward the roof of the building, she noticed it's distinctive design. The roof consisted of two wide, triangular cupolas, flanking a taller one in the center. Large cutout letters on the center cupola spelled out the word, 'CASINO.' Just below that, more cutout letters advertised the restaurant inside.

He seemed to notice her looking at the place. "Oh, there's a casino here. I didn't know that."

She shrugged. "I work in a saloon, I see poker games and gambling all the time. I'm far more interested in the Conservatory."

So they moved on, until they reached the front lawn of the Conservatory of Flowers. She craned her neck to look up at the structure, which sat a bit above them on a grassy slope. The center of the building was capped with a domed roof, and on each side of the central area was a long, narrow wing. The entire building was made of glass, with wooden supports, and the sunlight sparkling on the many windows made for a lovely sight.

Awe filled her. "My, it's impressive."

He agreed. "It is. It's the largest greenhouse for miles around, and I hear they have hundreds of varieties of flowers inside."

Still taking in the grand exterior, she could feel the smile spreading across her face. "Well for heaven's sake, let's go in and see them."

Hands still clasped, they went to the front entrance, where the door was opened for them by a worker inside. Once they'd tucked away the picnic basket and their coats in a room set aside for that purpose, they began to tour the interior. They opted to tour without a guide, so they could enjoy each other's company while they viewed the exhibits.

Navigating the paths of the greenhouse turned out to be quite entertaining. Each room boasted another grouping of exotic plants in full bloom. She inhaled the sweet fragrance hanging in the air as she explored all manner of rare orchids, succulents, and countless other flora. By the time they finished their tour, and stepped back out into the sunshine, she was convinced the Conservatory of Flowers was the most magical place she'd ever visited.

Shifting the basket around so he could grasp her hand again, he looked at her. "Did you enjoy that, dearest?"

"It was wonderful, and so was the company." She rose up on her toes to give him a peck on the cheek. The beauty of the day, and the sights and smells of all those magnificent flowers, had filled her with a sense of peace and contentment she'd not felt in a great while.

His answering smile belied his pleasure. "Tell me, what was your favorite flower?"

She pondered that difficult query for a few moments. "I think it would have to be the bearded Iris, the deep purple one. I've never seen one like that before, it was really lovely."

He nodded. "The sign said it was called the Plum Pudding, and that it came from Asia. I thought you might pick that one."

She stopped walking, looked up at him. "You remember all that?"

His dark eyes were as sincere as she'd ever seen them. "Sure. When I saw how you reacted to that flower, I knew I'd better take note."

Everything about his behavior today told her he was watching her, listening to her, and genuinely cared about her interests. Her smile broadened.

He chuckled. "You look mighty pleased."

"I am." She reached up to run her hand along his jaw.

Finding a nice, quiet spot away from the main walking trails, he withdrew a blanket from the basket he'd brought along and spread it out on the soft grass. Once they were seated there, she watched him open the basket and set out the food. There was a loaf of sliced bread, a wrapped bundle containing slices of roast turkey and tin of cookies. He'd also brought along two canteens filled with cool lemonade, and a small bottle of mustard for their sandwiches.

As he set a tin plate in front of her, she looked to him.

"This is all very sweet, Gregory. What kind of cookies did you bring?"

"They're shortbread cookies, from Ruby's."

She clapped her hands together. "My favorites! Let me guess...my aunt told you?"

He shook his head. "Not this time. When I went by to order our basket, Ruby added them in and told me how much you loved them."

She shook her head, smiling. It seemed as if at least a few folks in town were rooting for their relationship to work out. Knowing that, she could ignore the naysayers and gossips who didn't approve.

Once each had fixed themselves a sandwich from the offerings, they sat next to each other on the blanket and ate. The spot he'd pick was shaded by the canopy of trees above them, and somewhat secluded. After they'd eaten, and enjoyed the lemonade and cookies, he tucked the remains of it back into the basket.

He got to his feet. "Stand for a moment, would you?"

She did as he asked, watching as he rearranged things. He set the basket aside, and moved the blanket so it rested on the ground right near the base of a poplar tree. Then he sat down, leaning his back against the tree, with his long legs stretched out in front of him.

He opened his arms and cast his gaze in her direction.

She took the silent invitation, moving to where he sat. She eased down onto his lap, stretching her own legs out perpendicular to his. He wrapped his arms around her waist, and she leaned her head on his shoulder.

For a time they simply sat, enjoying the fresh breeze and the warmth of each other's bodies. The quiet in their little hamlet was only interrupted by the occasional murmur of conversation from other park goers passing by.

Sitting with him, enjoying the quiet and the comfort of his embrace, she could feel her heart opening to him. He didn't press her for anything, like some of the other men she'd courted; in fact, he seemed very content just holding her. She felt at home in his arms, as if this was the place she'd always been meant to be. The sounds of his breaths, the rise and fall of his chest, and the pounding of his heart seemed to sync with her own.

She could not recall a time when she'd felt this way about another man. He did something to her, something she didn't have the words to describe. Whatever it was, it felt marvelous. She wanted more of it, more of this serenity and bliss; as much as he was willing to give her.

He touched her cheek with caressing fingertips.

She raised her head, looked into his dark eyes. His intense gaze told her she held his singular focus, and it pierced her to the soul.

No words were spoken. None were needed.

His fingertips stroked along her jawline, then he guided her face toward his kiss.

The moment her lips touched, she bloomed inside, much like the exotic bearded iris. His tongue parted her lips and she melted as their tongues danced against each other. His mouth tasted of the tart lemonade and the sugary sweetness of the cookies. Her hands went to his sides, gripping the fabric of his dark jacket as the kiss intensified. She saw dancing flames, she saw swirling sparks. Her body felt as if were being seared by hot pokers. Between her legs, a subtle throbbing began, spreading and radiating to her extremities. The kiss lengthened and the throbbing grew more insistent. He felt the charge flowing between them, as evidenced by the hardness she felt beneath her hips.

Finally, she broke the seal of their lips. When she opened her eyes, she found him watching her.

She felt breathless, and if his own ragged breathing was any indicating, he'd been affected as well.

He stroked her face again, this time moving his fingertips along her hairline, in front of her ear. "Angel May, we must stop or..." he didn't finish his sentence, and he didn't have to.

She nodded. She knew what he wanted to say, knew what he was feeling because she felt it as well. The delicious, carnal heat sparking between them had been stoked just now. In that moment, the woman inside of her wanted to throw caution and morals to the wind, and take him somewhere where they could make slow, passionate love. But it was not to be, at least not yet.

She rose from her seat on his lap, took a few steps back in effort to put some distance between them. She would never have guessed their attraction would be so hot, so combustible, and she'd been wholly unprepared.

He stood as well, folded the blanket and replaced it in the basket. He then took off the dark suit jacket, tucking that into the basket as well. From the pocket of the crisp, wheat colored shirt, he drew out his pocket watch and looked at its face. "If we're to make the evening ferry we need to get back to the pier."

"Thank you again for bringing me here, Gregory."

He gathered the basket and held out his hand to her. "You're welcome. Since you enjoyed it so much, I hope to bring you again."

She slipped her hand into his. "You'll get no argument from me."

He started walking, and she followed close behind.

Kianna Alexander

Chapter 9

Angel sank into the soft cushion of the armchair, with an open issue of the Tribune on her lap. It was Thursday evening, the only evening this week she could get away from the saloon. She rarely spent much time at the Taylor Hotel, but she was meeting Gregory this evening for what he'd described as a "tryst." Unable to pass up such an enticing invitation, she'd agreed, and now was waiting for him in the lobby.

Folks were coming and going all around her. Visitors with their valises were moving about, checking in at the desk with Mr. Taylor, or being shown to their rooms by one of the Taylor children. There was foot traffic moving in and out of the dining room, as well as a few other folks sitting in the armchairs around her, reading or chatting with one another.

When he came downstairs, she sucked in a breath. Suddenly the bustling room seemed to fade away. He looked so handsome in his tight fitting denims and blue shirt. His dark locks were combed into place, and he carried his black Stetson in his hand. The hat matched the black boots on his feet. As he strode toward her, she admired the powerful muscles in his thighs. Glory, he was easy on the eyes.

He approached her and stuck out his hand. She took it, and held fast to it as they left the noisy confines of the hotel. Outside on the plank walk, she let him lead her north, up Town Road, past Ruby's eatery.

The evening air hung thick and heavy with humidity. Inhaling deeply, she could detect the scent of the rainstorm to come.

"Rain's coming soon."

His eyes were shadowed by the brim of his Stetson, but she

could see the slight smile on his lips. "I know. We'll be fine under the shelter, though."

They crossed the strip of grass adjacent to Ruby's, which lead to the town's picnic grounds. Last spring, Rod Emerson and his workers had built a large shelter, as a means for sheltering the townsfolk from elements if the weather turned rocky during an event. The shelter, with it's plank floor, four timber pillars, and shingled roof, now housed the six picnic tables that once dotted the grounds.

He stepped up from the grass onto the plank floor of the shelter, then helped her do the same. She then joined him at one of the tables. At this hour, they were the only ones there. Sitting next to him on the bench, she took in their surroundings. The leaves of the old trees, and the autumn gold grass, swayed in the breeze. A few yards away, she could see the water rippling on the surface of Hibbit's Pond.

Gregory's voice penetrated her thoughts."You were quite the rabblerouser at the debate."

She sighed, wishing he hadn't brought that up. Having already spent part of the day talking about the election with her girlfriends, she was in no mood to rehash the subject. "I merely spoke the truth. Nathan Greer is a chauvinist of the worst kind. Still, I don't want to talk about that anymore."

He tipped his hat up a bit, allowing her to see his piercing dark eyes. "Then I won't trouble you with it. What do you wish to talk about?"

By now, the rain came on. It was light, the small droplets falling softly over the windswept grass.

She watched him, letting her their gazes connect. His eyes held desire, smoldering like coals in a grate. She reached out, let her fingertips trace the hard outline of his jaw. "Not a thing."

He took her cue, and draped an arm around her waist, pulling her upper body closer to his own. A breath later, he pressed his lips to hers.

Kianna Alexander

The kiss was sweet, yet held a passionate urgency that made her core melt. Her lips parted, and his tongue slid inside her mouth. That turned the kiss even more hot, more needy. Her arms looped around his neck, and she felt him pull her onto his lap.

She went without protest, craving the warmth of his body against hers.

He broke the kiss once she was seated atop him. His dark, intense eyes swept over her body, while his hands caressed the outline of her breasts, confined inside her shirtwaist. As she arched to his touch, she cursed the infernal thing for denying her the full magic of his fingertips against her skin.

"My God, you're a beauty." He punctuated his words by placing a soft kiss in the hollow of her neck. Another kiss followed, then another, until the kisses melted into a series of soft licks, traveling the expanse of her bared shoulder, moving south toward the tops of her breasts.

Her soft sigh rose over the sound of the rain as her body responded to his attentions. His big hands resting on the small of her back served to steady her. The other hand dazzled her, lazily touring the curve of her skirt clad hip.

Never had a man touched her this way, so gently, so masterfully. It was as if he sought to push her into madness, and as he slid his caressing hand up her side and used it to free one of her breasts, she thought he might succeed.

She shivered as her breast was exposed to the cool, rain damp air. Watching him with wide eyes, she knew she should stop him; at any moment someone could happen by and be scandalized by their activities. But as his hot mouth closed over her nipple, any thoughts of stopping him disappeared. He suckled her, and her eyes slid closed against the blinding bliss.

He was hard for her. She could feel that part of him pressing against her bottom like a length of iron. Caught up in the sensation of him sucking and licking her hardened nipples, she moved her hips against it.

In response, a low, rumbling groan escaped his throat, and he eased away from her nipple. "Angel May, if you keep that up, I will turn your hips up across this table and have you."

Her body rippled with desire at his gruff words. The fog of passion lifted from her a bit, and rationality crept in. As much as the idea of making love with him appealed to her, she knew this wasn't the right time or place. She wasn't exactly a proper lady of society. Running a saloon precluded that. Still, whatever reputation she did possess would be dragged through the mud if they were caught trysting in public. Aside from that, Gregory would lose his job, ruin any chance of ever becoming sheriff, and likely be run out of town on a rail.

A look came over his handsome face, one that told her he was regaining his good sense, as well. He drew a deep breath as he gently tucked her breast back into the corset, then righted her shirtwaist. "Forgive me, Angel. There's something about you that hinders my good judgment, sweetheart."

Hearing the endearment made heat fill her cheeks, and she stroked his jaw. "I could say the same about you, Gregory. No apologies are needed."

He grasped her hand, sprinkling it with soft kisses. "I do want to continue this. Just not here."

She straightened, shifting off of his lap. "I agree. What's happening between us can't be denied." Her body still tingled from his touch and his kisses.

He was silent for a moment. Then, his expression turned serious. "I don't want to deceive you, Angel. My intentions aren't for marriage."

She shrugged, kept her face impassive. "There's no reason we can't enjoy this thing sparking between us."

"Is that so? And what would you call it, exactly?"

"Desire. Wanting. It's only natural between a man and a woman." She was no innocent, and she knew full well the special joy that could be found in the arms of man with a talent for all things carnal. She sensed the heat he possessed, and she wanted to experience it, even if it didn't lead to her becoming Mrs. Simmons.

He seemed skeptical. "So you'll make love with me, even though you know I don't want a wife?"

She hesitated. Should she tell him that she did want marriage, that she was falling in love with him? Exposing her heart to possible pain that way didn't sit well with her. So she chose to play into his sentiment. "I've made a life on my own for many years now, and I like it just fine."

He ran his hand over his chin, as if thinking over her words. "Then we're agreed. We'll enjoy each other's company, but that will be the balance of it."

She smiled, knowing it didn't reach her eyes. "Yes. That sounds wonderful."

He kissed her on the cheek.

She turned her face to his, and kissed his lips, before sprinkling a few kisses around his jawline. "I want you, Gregory, and I'm not sure how much longer I can wait."

He groaned again."Then name a time and place, my dear, and I'll be there."

"Sunday evening, at my apartment. Say, around seven?"

He nodded. "My shift ends at six. I'll be there."

"Good." Already, her body tingled with anticipation of the pleasure she would undoubtedly experience with this rugged, well-built man.

He stood, offered his arm. "Come. I'll walk you home."

She rose, linked her arm with his. They shared one more sweet kiss, then stepped out into the misty rain.

***

Saturday morning found Buck's Barbershop crowded with men, looking to get their weekly shaves and trims. Gregory sat in one of the chairs lined against the wall next to the door, which was propped open to allow in the fresh air.

The interior of the barbershop smelled of cigar smoke and aftershave. The exposed timbers that comprised the walls held little decoration, other than the sign that alerted newcomers to Buck's prices, a dartboard, and the rail of hooks for hanging hats. The sawdust floor was kept clean, and uncluttered by any fancy rugs. There were no lace curtains by the windows facing Founder's Avenue, no frilly doilies on the backs of the old rough hewn oak chairs. Buck's Barbershop lacked all traces of the so-called "woman's touch".

Two of the waiting men had turned their chairs and placed a barrel between them, and were playing a spirited hand of cards. Another fellow was engrossed in the reading of a leather bound book, and yet another was catching twenty winks as he waited for his turn in the barber's chair.

Next to Gregory, Noah reclined with his newspaper and a cup of coffee. Every one of the five other seats were occupied, as were both of Buck's barbering chairs. Buck's apprentice, Levell, worked on Saturdays to help stem the tide of customers.

Gregory asked, "How's the missus? Haven't seen her around lately."

Noah took a swig of coffee. "Fine, fine. She just hasn't been out much lately. She is complaining of being tired though. I think she might be carrying again."

He nodded. "You ready for another one?"

"If she's carrying, I don't have much choice, do I?" He lowered the paper to give him a wink, then raised it again. "Heard from your pa lately?"

"Yeah. Got a letter from him yesterday. He says crops are good, Ma is keeping busy with her church meetings, and they're still waiting for me to find a wife and settle down."

"Still riding you about that, eh?

He groaned at the thought. "Yes. Ever since Jack married four years ago, Ma and Pa have been on me and Luke to do the same." His brother Jack was two years his senior, and

Luke was four years younger. His parents' fondest wish seemed to be to see all their sons married off and saddled with wives and children, as soon as possible. Gregory wasn't sure he was so inclined. To his mind, there was nothing missing from his life. He had his work, his freedom, and his room over at the Taylor. What more did a man need, really?

"Don't worry. Eventually they'll leave you be."

Gregory hoped for his sanity's sake Noah was right. He leaned back in his chair, letting his head drop back to rest against the wall.

Noah, his face still hidden behind the open pages of the Ridgeway Tribune, nudged him with his elbow. "Hey, Greg. Have you seen this so-called Murchison Letter?"

Taking a sip from his own mug of coffee, he shook his head. "Nope. Haven't read this week's edition yet."

Buck, working his shears on the head of town blacksmith and liveryman Henry Carl, commented, "I haven't read it yet, either. What's the story, Noah?"

Noah folded his paper and set it on his lap. "McCormack picked the story up from the AP wire and ran it. Seems a British man named Charles F. Murchison, living here in California, wrote a letter to the British Ambassador Slackville."

Henry shrugged. "What's that got to do with anything?"

Noah cut him a look. "Hell, Henry, let me finish, will ya? Anyhow, this Murchison fellow wanted advice from the ambassador on who he should vote for in the presidential race."

Gregory smiled. "So there's the rub. What did the old Brit say?"

Noah grinned. "Sir Slackville has thrown his support behind Cleveland. Says he's the best man for British interests."

A series of grunts and groans, and few chuckles, could be heard around the shop.

Buck brushed the fallen hair off Henry's shoulders. "Well,

that ought to seal it for Harrison, then!"

More laughter followed that observation.

Gregory shook his head. He still hadn't decided who he'd vote for, or if he'd even bother to cast a ballot. Either way, listening to his buddies talk politics always amused him.

One of the card playing men stood as Buck gestured him toward a chair. "Well, my vote's going with Cleveland either way."

Buck asked, "Why would you throw your support behind the man the Brits like?"

The man shook his head as he slid into Buck's chair. "To hell with the Brits, and who they like. All I know is my brother works for a shipping company in San Fran. He says if the tariffs goes any higher, he's likely gonna be out of a job. Boss man can't keep the outfit open at these rates, and Harrison'll only raise 'em more."

Levell, the youngest man in the shop at nineteen, cleared his throat. "Cleveland's against pensions for veterans of the Great War. My granddad, my pa, and my uncle served bravely for the Union. Far as I'm concerned, Cleveland's full o' horse shit."

Raucous laughter filled the room.

Buck slapped his apprentice on the back. "He don't say much, but when he do open up his mouth, watch out!"

Gregory shook his head, laughing along with the rest of his buddies. The boy was shy, but also pretty damn smart. "What about that other guy- the brigadier general. Haven't heard much about him."

Noah scratched his chin. "Oh, yeah. Clinton Fisk is his name. Served with the boys in blue during the war. He's done a lot of good work in the South, as I hear it- Freedman's schools and such. But I don't expect him to go far."

Gregory asked, "Why not?"

"He's running for the Prohibition party."

Buck nearly dropped his shears. "What? A man, a veteran

at that, and he don't want us to be able to have a cold brew now and again?"

Noah chuckled. "Told ya he won't get far."

The other man who'd been playing card suddenly spoke up. "You're one to talk, Noah. You and your deputy there are in cahoots with the women."

The talk and laughter fell silent for a moment. Only the sound of Buck's shears could be heard.

Gregory narrowed his eyes at the fellow, who looked familiar, but wasn't someone he knew well. "What do you mean, in cahoots? You off your rocker or something?"

The man pressed on. "Noah's out campaigning for 'em to get the vote, as if they got enough sense, and you're sniffing behind the barmaid like she's the last piece of tail 'tween here and Mexico."

Someone whistled.

Next to him, Noah stiffened. "Look here. You just better watch your mouth, before you start any trouble."

The man, unrelenting in what seemed like a quest to get Gregory's goat, stood, and pointed his finger at him. "I'm not the one who lets some barmaid go around with his balls in her handbag."

Gregory was on his feet in a flash.

Buck's eyes widened. "Oh, hell."

Noah got up and sidled away, nearly tripping over the man napping in his chair.

Gregory took a couple of long steps to the where the man stood, and grabbed him by the shirtfront. The other man being a good seven or eight inches shorter, and forty pounds lighter, Gregory had no trouble lifting him until his feet left the floor.

All activity in the room stopped. The singing of the metal shears ceased as Buck and Levell quit their barbering to watch the fracas unfold.

Dangling the man a few feet above the floor, Gregory spoke through gritted teeth. "You seem mighty concerned about my personal business. What goes on between me and Miss Lane ain't none of your concern. Did you come here for a shave, or to have your teeth shoved up into your empty head?"

Trembling visibly, the man located his voice. "..C...C...Came for a s..sh..shave."

"Good. Then keep your mouth shut and you might stay conscious long enough to get one." Gregory let go of the man's shirt, letting him fall in a heap on the sawdust floor.

The man got up, dusted himself off a bit. Red-faced, he got his deck of cards and went to the door.

Before he left, he spoke. "You'll see. Those women are gonna learn their place. One way or the other."

Then he was gone.

Buck broke the silence. "Damn it, Greg, you just cost me a customer. You owe me five dollars."

Gregory shook his head as he returned to his seat. "I'll gladly pay it, rather than listen to that jackass."

Noah, now moving into Levell's chair for his trim, whistled. "I'd haul you in for assault, but he had it coming."

"Damn straight. He was asking for it. He'd just better be glad I didn't kick his ass." He leaned back in his chair and blew out a pent up breath. As a law officer, he tried to keep his temper in check, so he could do his job without worry of making costly mistakes. But that fellow had tested his patience a little too much by making all those declarations about what went on between him and Angel.

By the time he'd had his turn in the chair, his anger had faded enough for him to recall the stranger's words as he left the barber shop.

Those women are gonna learn their place, one way or the other.

It hadn't been a threat, exactly, but Gregory felt an innate mistrust for the man. His cryptic words made him feel unease, and as a lawman, he knew to trust his instincts over all else. From now on, until the election proceedings were finished, he'd be keeping a sharp eye out for any sign of trouble from Mr. Big Mouth.

If that fellow decided to bring trouble to Ridgeway, Gregory would make sure he regretted it.

Chapter 10

Sunday morning, Angel rose early; but not as early as her aunt. When she emerged from her bedroom, still rubbing her sleep-heavy eyes, she found Myrna seated on the settee, tucking a few items into her valise. She'd been planning for a few weeks now to visit an old friend in Oakland.

Inhaling the aroma of the coffee her aunt had made, Angel greeted her. "Good morning Aunt Myrna."

"Morning, dear. Hustle, now. I've got to be at the depot in an hour."

Stifling a yawn, she nodded, and went to get a little coffee. After she'd gotten a bit of the brew in her system, she put on a pair of moccasins, then slipped a muslin cloak on over her simple skirt and blouse.

Aunt Myrna got to her feet, valise in hand. "Ready?"

She nodded, and escorted her aunt out the rear door. The saloon was closed, as it always was on Sundays, so they walked around the Taylor Hotel, then crossed the street and headed for the depot.

The newly built Transit Depot sat on the far eastern edge of town, just beyond the livery on Founder's Avenue. For now, it served as a hub for folks traveling via stagecoach, or those wanting to rent horses or vehicles. The nearest train station was in Oakland, and the Transit Depot provided a connection to the train route, as well as transportation to those other small cities not located along the route.

Angel carried her aunt's valise and escorted her right up to the door.

Ever the independent spirit, Myrna tried to wave her off."You don't have to wait with me, dear. I'll be perfectly fine until the stage comes."

"I know. But I'd like to see you off, and make sure you get on the stage safely." She led her aunt to a bank of chairs near the depot's doors, and they sat.

"I can't wait to see Sam. It's been such a long time." Myrna smiled, her eyes holding a wistful look.

She watched her aunt's body language as she spoke of her friend. Angel didn't know anything about Sam, except that her aunt had met her years ago during her days on the stage. "She must really be something. "

"That she is. In a lot of ways, she reminds me of your mother."

A moment passed between them in silence, and they shared the pain of missing her. Lucille Lane had been vitally important to both of them.

Angel squeezed her shoulders. "Now I know she's something special. Heavens, I miss Mama."

Myrna sighed. "I miss her too, dear."

She held back the tears that threatened to fall.

A chuckle escaped Myrna's lips as she said, "Do you remember the year you asked your mother for your first corset?"

A smile stretched her lips as she recalled that summer. "Yes. I had just turned thirteen, and was coming into my bosom."

"And your mother knew that. She and I had been talking about what to do. You were growing into your figure and your mama was just beside herself about it."

"I remember. When I asked her, she just kept saying, 'my baby, my baby.' Then she fainted!"

Myrna was in full laughter now, leaning forward and slapping her thigh.

Angel joined her, because telling the story always seemed to tickle her. As a girl of thirteen, Angel had been downright determined to get a corset as a sign that she was a "woman." Now that she was grown, she couldn't abide the uncomfortable, confining garment. She hated corsets so much she couldn't remember the last time she'd worn one.

She looked over at her aunt, who was just now recovering

from her amusement. Angel loved her aunt Myrna dearly, and part of the reason was this; their shared memories of her mother. They were the only two people left in the world who'd been fortunate enough to know Lucille Lane, to experience her gentle spirit, and to love her.

Once the stagecoach arrived, and Aunt Myrna and her valise were safely inside, Angel crossed the street and went back to her apartment. Alone inside the space, she drew a deep breath. Tonight, Gregory was coming over. Already, her body tingled with anticipation of what they would share. For now, she needed to get her apartment, and herself, ready for what she was sure would be a wonderful evening.

Yesterday, before she'd gone to the debate, she'd visited the beauty parlor. Christina, the town hairdresser, had fashioned her hair into the style that Gregory seemed to find so attractive. Angel planned to wear her hair down tonight, to symbolize the intimacy she hoped to share with him.

She spent the afternoon sweeping up and making sure her apartment was tidy. Since Gregory would be coming from a long day at work, she heated up the wood stove, and prepared a small hen, along with some diced potatoes and carrots. As she slid the pan inside and closed the oven, it occurred to her that this was the first time she'd ever cooked for a man.

While their dinner cooked, she went into her bedroom to choose the perfect gown, one that would tempt him with the promise of a very decadent dessert.

She flipped through everything in her wardrobe, and finally settled on a dark gown the color of plums. She'd never worn it before, since she favored trousers. Something told her that the cut of the dress, with its shoulder baring top, would appeal to her man.

She smiled at the possessive way she thought of him as she slipped into the gown, foregoing undergarments. They didn't agree on much, but their attraction was so strong, it could no longer be denied.

She was taking the roast hen out of the oven when the knock sounded on her apartment door. She quickly deposited the pan atop the stove and dashed to the door to let him in.

When she opened the door, Gregory stood there, smiling. He held a bouquet of colorful blooms, which she briefly regarded before letting her eyes sweep over his tall, muscular frame. He wore a white shirt beneath his brown leather vest, and a pair of denims that hugged his hips. He took off his Stetson, the dark eyes connecting with hers. "Evenin', Angel May.

The sight of him standing there threatened to take her breath away. She nodded a greeting, unable to speak.

His smile broadened, as if he sensed her weakness and found it endearing. "Do you want me to stay out here?"

She blinked a few times, released a nervous titter as she stepped back to allow him entry. "Sorry. Come in."

He moved into the apartment and she shut the door behind him. She watched as he took off his hat and vest, placing them on the old oak coat rack by the door.

"Something smells good." His remark cut through the silence.

"I thought you might be hungry after working all day. I roasted a hen with some potatoes and carrots."

"A beautiful companion, and a meal. I'm a lucky man." He closed the space between them. Touching her chin, he lifted her face up and placed a soft kiss on her lips.

Her cheeks heated at his words. Her whole body felt warm; his very presence seemed to heat her blood. "You're quite the charmer this evening."

"Only for you, dear." He kissed her again, this time on the cheek.

Sensing the growing heat between them, she gave him a nudge. "Come. Let's eat before the food gets cold."

Kianna Alexander

She walked to the kitchen with him only a breath behind her. Gesturing for him to take a seat, she set about carving the hen. When she presented him with a plate, piled with half the hen and the roasted vegetables, he clapped his hands together.

"Thank you for the meal, Angel. It looks marvelous."

She passed him a cup of lemonade, then sat down with her own food. "I hope you like it."

For a time, only the sounds of their silverware striking the china plates filled the apartment. She glanced up to see him eating heartily, and that pleased her.

"How was work today? Anything interesting happen?" She was pretty sure that if a crime had taken place she would have heard about it by now, but she wanted him to know she cared about his work.

He shook his head, swallowing a mouthful of roast hen. "No. Just a typical day filing reports, making patrols, that sort of thing."

She nodded. "All I did today was see my aunt onto the stagecoach to Oakland. I usually take it pretty easy when the saloon is closed."

The finished the meal in companionable silence. He pushed his plate away, patting his stomach with a satisfied grin. "Angel May, thank you again for that delicious meal."

She felt the smile stretching her lips. "I'm glad you enjoyed it. I've got a strawberry tart in the icebox, if you have room for dessert."

He reached across the table to grasp her hand. His dark eyes were alive with desire as he spoke. "Honey, you are the only dessert I want."

Her pulse quickened, her breath catching in her throat.

He stood, walked around the table, his hand still wrapped around hers. Gently he urged her to her feet, He ran his fingertips along her jawline, then showered torrid kisses across the bared expanse of her shoulders. "Will you give me the dessert I'm craving, Angel?"

Kianna Alexander

"Yes..." The word escaped her lips on a breathless sigh as he continued to brush his lips against the sensitive nook of her neck. In that moment, she'd have done anything he asked.

Her knees weakened, turning to jelly as he kissed the tops of her breasts, bared by the cut of her gown. She braced her hips against the table to keep from sinking to the floor in a heap.

His bold hands reached inside the top of the gown to free her breasts. His dark eyes glittered with desire. He moved his hands to cup the twin globes, bent his head to pleasure them with his warm mouth.

"Ah." Her head lolled back when his lips closed over one of her nipples. He let his tongue bathe it, then drew several long, deep sucks before moving his magical attentions to the other nipple.

Now the sighs escaped her one after another. Her whole world was spinning, all rational thought drowned out by the dizzying pleasure he brought.

Finally he pulled away. She looked at him, found him watching her.

With desire blazing like a fire alarm fire in his eyes, he said, "Come. Let's go to your bed."

His arm moved around her waist and she went willingly, letting him guide her and her disheveled gown into her bedroom.

***

Gregory could not recall ever being so hard and so ready to please a woman as he was at this moment. Angel lay across the bed, with the bodice of the deep purple gown in disarray. Her pert brown breasts, capped with dark nipples left hard and begging by his earlier attentions, were bared to his hungry eyes. The dark riches of her hair were spread out around her head, her lips were kiss swollen. Her tawny eyes were focused on him, and held an invitation he could not resist even if he wanted to.

He moved his body to position himself between her legs, where they dangled off the side of the bed. His manhood throbbed, and all he wanted was to ruck up the dress, strip away her underthings, and bury himself deep between her rich golden thighs. He held himself in check. This night was their first encounter, and he wanted to take his time gifting her with more pleasure than she'd ever experienced before.

He leaned low to place a soft kiss on her lips. "Let's get you out of this gown."

Her only reply was a soft, sultry smile.

He stood again. He grasped one of her ankles, then led his hand slide up the silken skin of her leg. When he reached her thigh and found it bare, he drew a sharp breath.

"You're nude underneath." He stated it instead of asking her, because his hands were already touring the warm softness of her naked flesh beneath the flowing skirts.

Her eyes tempted him to explore further. "I thought you might be pleased to discover that."

He groaned low in his throat while rucking up the gown, pushing the skirts into a bundle around her waist. The full expanse of her bronze legs was revealed to his hot gaze, and his attention went immediately to the triangle of curls crowning her shapely thighs. A moment passed with him simply admiring the beauty of her body. His manhood was now so engorged he feared he might spill before he removed his trousers.

He knew he had to remove the last, silken barrier between him and her body, lest he ruin the gown. He reached for her hands, helped her to her feet.

She showed him her back, and he worked as quickly as he could to undo what seemed like a hundred tiny buttons and loops running down the dress. When he finally finished, the open halves fell apart to her waist. He stepped back a bit to allow her to remove it. Before his very appreciative eyes, she shimmied the garment down her hips and let it pool around her ankles before stepping out of it. The moment she did, he turned her to face him, his hands cupped the round softness of her bottom. He caressed her, gave her gentle squeezes as he drew her close, kissing her lips.

By now his body demanded release, so he eased her away from him, and helped her lie back across the bed. He shed his own clothing hastily, then joined her on the bed. Their bodies touched as he lay next to her, kissing her lips and letting his hands tour the curves of her nude flesh.

"You are beautiful." The words slipped from his lips on an awe filled whisper, then the kisses began anew. He took his time making her ready to receive all he had to give, placing slow, languid kisses between her breasts, and down the soft plane of her stomach. Her sighs were like music to his ears as he eased his way between her thighs. When he placed his kisses there, her back arched like a bow and her legs fell open to allow him full access to the very center of her. He remained there, stroking her with his lips and tongue, until release shattered her and she cried out his name.

He moved above her, enjoying the sight of pleasure's glow on her face. Bracing himself on one elbow, he cupped her bottom with the other hand and slid smoothly into her. Her body accepted him readily, and when she began to clench around him, he brought his hands to her waist and held on. Then he started to rock his hips, letting his passion have its full head.

Moving in and out of her at increasing speed, he felt himself hardening even more. Her silken warmth pushed him to the very heights of arousal. Holding back became more difficult, then impossible. He pressed his upper body against her soft breasts, lifted her hips with both hands, and stroked her like a man gone mad.

The soft moans slipping from her lips became louder, more intense as he made love to her. Soon his own groans filled the room, harmonizing with hers like their very own passionate music.

Kianna Alexander

She shattered then, her silken passage quivering and compressing him as she cried out his name.

Her crisis fueled his own. On a shout of glory, he gave one last thrust as his whole body vibrated with ecstasy. Everything in his body sang her name as he lay atop her, folding her into his embrace. With their bodies still joined, he showered her face with soft kisses until sleep swept him away.

Gregory opened his eyes, taking a moment to let them adjust to the dim light of Angel's bedroom. He raised his head from the feather pillow a bit, listening.

He heard only her soft, breathy snores.

As if she sensed his scrutiny, she opened her eyes. Sleepily, she looked to him. "What is it? Why are you watching me like that?"

He looked at her, lying there among the rumpled bedclothes. The glimmer of light from the rising sun cast a golden light on her, making her look as angelic as her name implied. She'd taken his heart, and he couldn't bear the thought of a life without her.

That moment, he knew he would do whatever he must to protect her.

"Angel, you're going to have to take some measures to ensure your safety."

Her round eyes found his. "Like what?"

"Like, never walking alone after dark. And making your doors are locked at night. As a matter of fact, I'm going to the mercantile to get you a new set of bolts for your doors, and ..."

She stuck up her hand. "Hold on, Greg. I've walked around town after dark alone for years, and I'm perfectly capable of taking care of myself."

He shook his head. "I'm telling you, Angel. You've got to take precautions. Lupe can walk with you places, or one of your other trouble-making friends. It doesn't matter to me so long as you aren't out alone."

She rolled her eyes, crossing her slender arms over her bosom. "Would you listen to yourself? You can't tell me what to do, Gregory. You're not my Pa, and you're certainly not my husband."

He could feel his brow furrowing. Why was she being so contrary? All he wanted was to ensure her safety. "Come now, Angel. Why can't you just do as I say, honey?"

"Oh, do you mean like last night, when you didn't want me on top of you?"

He pressed his hand to his temple, feeling his head begin to throb. In the wee hours of darkness, she'd awakened him for a second round of lovemaking, and he had insisted she lie beneath him. Was she really holding that against him? He did all the work, leaving her nothing but the leisurely enjoyment of their coupling.

"Well?" Her eyes flashed angrily.

"The natural way of lovemaking means the man is on top..."

"And in control. Go on and say it, Gregory. That's what you really want. To be in control, all the time, in every situation."

He blew out a breath. "Angel May, that's not what..."

"Stifle, Greg. I don't want to hear it. Best thing for you to do right now is get your gear and leave."

He stared at her. "Are you serious? You're throwing me out?"

She didn't flinch. "How can I make myself any more clear? Get out, Gregory."

With a groan, he slipped his feet into his boots, then stood. Fastening his gun belt and putting his sidearm into it, he looked at her again. Surely she would come to her senses at any moment.

The frown marring her face told him that wasn't going to happen. She stood, still holding the sheet around her body. "Go on, scoot!"

He strode into the parlor, got his vest and hat from the

coat rack. As he shrugged into the vest he shot her a censuring look. "I'm only thinking of what's best for you, you know."

She harrumphed. "And you presume to know what's best, as always. Get out, and don't come back until you've gotten over your delusions of male superiority."

She held open the door and nudged him out before slamming it in his face.

Outdone, he turned and started walking toward Buck's. Knowing his friend, he'd have a cigar, and after dealing with his prickly little vixen, he could certainly use a smoke.

Chapter 11

Angel moved slowly down the toiletry aisle of the mercantile, tucking her purchases into the canvas bag she'd gotten at the counter. Lupe trailed behind her with a bag of her own.

Tucking a lavender scented bar of soap into her bag, she turned to Lupe. "Can you believe Gregory thought he was going to tell me what I should and should not do?"

Lupe, examining a package of bath salts, rolled her eyes. "He's a man. That's how they are."

"Well, no man in my life is going to be that way, because I won't have it."

Lupe chuckled, dropping her voice to a whisper. "Oh, please. If he's as talented in bed as you say he is, you'll let him get away with plenty."

Angel said nothing in response to that, but Lupe's words did bring back a flood of heated memories of Gregory's loving. He was a well made man, and he knew a plethora of ways to make her body sing his name. A tingle danced down her spine as she recalled the feel of his big hands and soft lips all over her body.

Another shopper turned sideways and squeezed down the aisle to pass them, reminding Angel that she was in public. She shook off the carnal memories as best she could, trying to focus instead on her shopping.

She was inspecting a bottle of perfumed toilet water when she heard a male voice.

"Well. If it isn't two of the most troublesome hellions in town."

The hairs on the back of her neck stood on end, and she whirled around to face Nathan Greer, who stood at the top of the aisle, smiling smugly as if he thought himself very clever. He was a short man, rail thin and dressed in a brown suit that did nothing for his pale coloring. His salt and pepper hair was beginning to recede, and the beady little brown eyes, hidden behind a pair of bronze rimmed spectacles, raked over her like grimy fingers.

"Hello to you, too, Mr. Greer. I see you still have the manners of someone raised in a cave."

A frown furrowed his woolly, graying brows. "Sass, as always. I'm not surprised. You never did know your place."

Lupe, her fists propped on her hips, lit into him. "Oh, go on with your fat mouth, Greer. We ain't interested in anything you have to say."

"Is that so? You may want to change your mind, because when I win the election, I'm going to see that your little sin palace is shut down."

Angel groaned. "I'm not interested in your threats, Greer."

He tugged his lapels in the self-important way that made Angel's blood boil. "It's no threat. As a matter of fact, closing the saloon will be my very first order of business. And after that, I'll be setting in motion some laws to keep you females in your..." he eyed the two of them with malice filled eyes..."natural place."

Lupe made a face as if she'd caught a whiff of something foul. Then she began muttering rapidly in Spanish, something she often did when angered.

Angel could feel her own face tightening. There was something about the way Greer was looking at her that made her skin crawl. He seemed to be regarding her with a mixture of hatred and lust, and it made her feel as if an entire colony of ants had taken up residence beneath her clothing.

Not bothering to mask her dislike for him, she turned on her heel, tossing back, "Have a good day, Mr. Greer." She moved away, with Lupe in tow.

"Don't you walk away from me, you little tart!"

She glared back at him. "This tart isn't under your command, so take your threats and jam them right up your hind end, you oaf!"

As he stood there, his jaw hanging open like an unlatched barn door, she and Lupe went to the counter to pay for their purchases.

He had sense enough not to approach them again, and Angel was glad of it.

As they stepped out onto the walk with their goods, Lupe adjusted her small flowered hat, then turned to her. "I don't know how Perry puts up with him. He's such a pain in the ass."

She chuckled at the mention of Greer's wife, Persephone. "I don't know either. Maybe she doesn't 'put up with him.' Maybe sleeping on the settee every night is why he's so damn ornery."

They both laughed at that.

"What were you saying in Spanish back there, Lupe?"

A small smirk crossed her face. "I was cursing him, which I'm sure you know. Anyhow I'd best not repeat it in English. Let's just say I called him some choice names."

She gave her friend a playful punch in the arm. "Naughty Lupe. Such language."

A silent beat passed between them, before Lupe spoke again.

"Do you really think he'd shut us down, Angel?"

"If he wins, I'm sure he'll do everything in his power to make our lives miserable. Not just us, but every woman in this town."

Lupe shook her head. "Dash it all. I wish we could vote, so we could vote against the bounder."

Angel kept her eyes on the walk ahead, being careful to avoid other people moving past her. "He's cocky, that's for sure. But don't worry. He can't do anything to us if he loses."

As she an Lupe moved on down the road, she pushed away thoughts of Nathan Greer, and any actions he might take if he were elected. Despite all his bluster, he hadn't won yet.

Kianna Alexander

They passed the corner near the library, and waited to cross the road. They stood there, unaware of the man watching them from behind the building that housed Lilly's Dress Emporium, and waited for traffic to slow.

When they crossed the street, the man waited a few beats, then followed them.

Lupe glanced back over her shoulder.

The man turned his back quickly, and headed north past the hotel while the girls headed east toward the saloon.

Angel, noticing Lupe's backward glance, said, "What is it, Lupe?"

She shook her head, refocusing her attention. "Nothing, I suppose."

The two women entered the saloon, letting the doors swing shut behind them.

***

Angel helped her aunt climb aboard the buggy seat, then walked around to climb up herself. Releasing the hand brake, she got the two horse team underway.

The early November night was cool and breezy, the air scented with the sap of the towering pines and spruce lining either side of the dark road. The lit lanterns hanging from either side of the buggy cast a soft glow on the hard packed earth beneath the wheels of the vehicle. Around them, only the sounds of the insects and frogs, and the rhythmic cadence of the horse's hooves, disturbed their companionable silence.

"So, what did you think of my quilting circle? Not as dull as you thought, eh?" Myrna tugged at afghan she's thrown over her lap.

Angel could only shake her head. "Not dull at all. I never dreamed you and your friends would talk that way."

Kianna Alexander

Myrna chuckled. "What, you didn't think old ladies talked about coupling? Come now, dear. We may be old, but we're not dead yet."

That made Angel let out a laugh of her own. She certainly had received an "education" on sex from the elderly ladies of town, one she hadn't been expecting. But she had to admit, even with their brash talk, the older women of town had a lot of wisdom to impart about relationships, motherhood, and life in general. It would probably be another month or more before she had time to attend another quilting circle meeting with her aunt, but she was already looking forward to it.

They moved at a steady pace up the road leading toward town, and home. No other vehicles were on the road, at least not within sight. Angel kept her focus on guiding Cocoa and Caramel, the two mares pulling them along.

Suddenly, the thundering sound of fast moving horses began to echo around them.

Myrna sat up a bit in the seat, turned her head to look behind them, in the direction of the sound. "Someone's in a mighty big hurry."

She agreed. "Sure sounds that way. Can you see them yet?"

"No, but I should any minute. They're coming on fast, whoever it is."

"Well, let me know when you see them, in case I need to pull over so they can hurry on by." Angel kept her eyes on the road ahead, knowing her first responsibility was to drive her own vehicle as safely as possible, even if others thought it prudent to ride their horses as if their tails were on fire.

The thundering became louder as the horses moved closer to them. Angel still didn't turn around, but she did feel a chill run down her spine.

There was something ominous in the air, a charge of negativity that made her feel unsafe.

As suddenly as the sensation came on, she heard a gunshot

ring out in the darkness.

Myrna shouted, "Good Lord, Angel! It's two riders, and their bearing down on us fast!"

She still didn't turn around- there was no need. All she wanted to do was put as much distance as she could between her buggy and the two lunatics on horseback. So she slapped the reigns, pushing Cocoa and Caramel to a run.

The buggy shook and shimmied as it picked up speed. Behind them, another shot rang out, followed by the shouts and hoots of the mounted men pursuing them.

"Get out of town, troublemaker!"

"Yeah! Run away, bitch!"

Angel didn't take kindly to being slurred, and a mixture of fear and anger heated her blood. She fought down the shivers running through her body, glanced over at her aunt. Myrna was pale faced, but looked angry as well. Angel decided in that moment that she would not allow those jackasses to harm her dear, sweet aunt. The woman hadn't lived nearly seventy years to be terrorized by the likes of them. With a shout of her own, Angel snapped the reins again, urging the horses on.

The buggy continued to wobble as the two mares charged down the road at full speed. With each stone or dip in the road they hit, both women were jostled around in the seat. The small buggy wasn't meant to be driven at such a high speed, but in this situation, there was no other option. Jaw set, Angel held tight to the reins. She could see the blacksmith's shop come into view, just a few hundred yards away, and she felt a modicum of relief. If she could make it into town, she'd ride straight up to the sheriff's office for help.

Behind her, the shooting stopped, but the men continued to yell all manner of threats and insults at them. She couldn't tell how far away they were, or if they might be gaining on the buggy. So she twisted her head for only a moment, to gauge their proximity.

Kianna Alexander

In that split second, the buggy ran over a fallen log laying across the road.

On impact, the buggy lurched violently, tossing Angel and Myrna to the right. Angel stuck her hand out, leveraging herself against the seat back to keep from sliding into her aunt. Then she whirled back around, struggled to regain control.

Myrna, wide eyed, shouted, "Heavens!"

Cocoa's harness snapped, and the horse continued at a run, leaving the buggy behind. Caramel yowled, and the vehicle veered off to the right side as the two left wheels lost contact with the surface of the road. They were jostled again as the buggy swung into the brush.

Angel screamed, reached out for her aunt.

The buggy overturned, tossing them both from the wooden seat like a pair of rag dolls.

She hit the ground on her back, landing in the damp grass with her aunt's frail form on top of her.

She tried to scream again, stuck her hands out to try to brace against what was coming.

But the buggy crashed down on top of them, plunging her world into thick, inky darkness.

Lupe pulled her cloak a bit tighter around her body as she walked up the road toward town. She'd agreed to come in early today to help Angel inventory the saloon's supply of spirits. Though the sun shone brightly, dappling the road's surface with the light filtering through the canopy of trees above, the morning air still held a chill.

About two hundred yards outside of town, something caught her eye. She took a moment to ascertain what she saw, and when realization hit her, she stopped dead in her tracks.

"Oh my Lord!"

She ran toward the overturned buggy, which lay in the brush and bramble on the right side of the road. The closer

she got to it, the more familiar the vehicle looked-
 Until she realized it was Angel's.
 She gasped, her hand flying to her mouth as tears sprang
to her eyes. Not wanting to get any closer, because she was
afraid of what she might find, she turned her feet toward
town again, and ran as fast as she could to get help.

Kianna Alexander

Chapter 12

Gregory pored over the the last of a stack of reports he'd been writing up, checking to be sure he'd included every pertinent detail. With his feet up on the big desk, he reclined comfortably, holding a quill pen in one hand as he reviewed the papers. Thaddeus was in the rear of the building, and he could hear the strokes of the broom as the young officer worked to clear the cells and hallway floors of dust and dirt.

He sat up, lay the paper on the surface of the desk, intent on affixing his signature. He dipped the tip of the pen in the inkwell.

Lupe ran in, screaming, "Angel's been hurt!"

He knocked the inkwell over as he jumped to his feet. His heart climbed into his throat. "What?"

Lupe, breathless and panting, leaned forward at the waist and placed her hands on her knees. "I was walking to work, and I found her buggy, overturned on the side of the road!"

He could hear his heart pounding in his ears as he hurried to grab his vest and hat from the hook above the desk. He called to his light horseman. "Thad! There's an emergency! Keep an eye on the place while I see to it."

Thad stuck his head around the corner, peering curiously at Lupe. "Yes, sir. But what's going on?"

Gregory was already donning his hat and stepping out the door with Lupe. "No time to explain now."

Outside on the walk, Gregory hurried around the corner to Doc Wilkins's clinic. The petite Lupe struggled to keep up with his long strides, but he couldn't slow down, not when he knew his Angel was in danger. His brow furrowed as disturbing thoughts entered his mind. How had the buggy come to be overturned? How long at it been there? Was she even still alive? Picturing her lying there, alone and injured in the cold, damp grass, threatened to be his undoing.

Once at the clinic, he pounded on the door.

The old bespectacled Doc Wilkins answered almost immediately. In his black medical coat and broadcloth trousers, he peered up at Gregory with concern lining his face. "Heavens, what's happened?"

Lupe spoke up. "Doc, come quick. Angel's buggy is upended on the side of the road at the edge of town."

Doc Wilkins' eyes widened. "I'll get my bag. Meet me out back at my buckboard."

He disappeared inside the clinic, and Gregory and Lupe did as he asked, rounding to the back of the small cabin-like structure to the spot where the doctor kept his buckboard parked. The vehicle was a simple one, with a seat accommodating two or three folks, and a flat bed in the back, suitable for hauling patients who were to infirm to sit up. On some sad occasions, the bed was used to haul the bodies of folks who'd expired, in absence of or despite the doctor's treatments. Looking into the bed of the vehicle, Gregory fought off the chill that coursed through him. *Will my sweet Angel May be taking that final ride?*

He glanced at Lupe, and from the pallor that had fallen over her face, he guessed she might be filled with the same sense of dread and foreboding.

The doctor came a few moments later, sliding his medical bag beneath the seat of the buckboard. He jogged over to the small barn that sat a few yards behind the clinic, and brought out his stallion. Once the beast was hitched and secured to the board, he climbed onto the seat.

Gregory helped Lupe aboard, and once she was seated next to the doctor, the deputy climbed up and took a seat.

Doc Wilkins slapped the reins, and they were off. He urged the stallion to a quick trot, and as they thundered through town, folks on the walk stopped what they were doing to watch them pass by. Everyone in town knew that when they saw Doc Wilkins hurrying down the road, there must be trouble. To that end, folks who were on the road slowed or halted their vehicles, and pulled out of his path to let him pass. Gregory coughed to clear his lungs of the swirling dust kicked up by the horse's pounding hooves and the rapidly spinning wheels of the buckboard.

It took only a few minutes for them to reach the spot Lupe pointed out. Before the Doc could bring his vehicle to a full stop, Gregory jumped down from the seat and ran over to the wrecked buggy.

When he reached it, he let his eyes scan the brush for any sign of Angel. He squatted near the buggy, opening his ears to listen for something, anything, that might indicate she was alive.

Then he heard it.

The shallow, shaky sounds of someone's uneven breaths. The sound emanated from beneath the overturned buggy.

He immediately searched for a handhold to lift the buggy, shouting, "Come on, Doc! She's underneath it, I can hear her!"

Doc Wilkins ran over and knelt beside him. Tossing the medical bag down in the grass, he too grabbed an edge of the buggy. Lupe joined in as well, placing her hands on the side opposite the doctor.

Gregory counted out loud. "One...two...three!"

With a mighty push, the three of them managed to lift the buggy. Gregory leaned into it hard with his shoulder. He managed to push it up and over until it was righted, just to the left of where it had overturned.

Sure enough, there was Angel, lying in the grass on her back. A few of the brass fittings from the buggy were scattered around her.

Seeing her bruised face made Gregory's breath catch. As he reached for her, moving her cloak aside to see if she were further injured, he gasped.

"Dear God," Lupe whispered.

There, on top of Angel, lay the frail and still body of her

aunt Myrna.

While noisy, rattling breaths were escaping from Angel, there wasn't a sound to be heard from the old woman.

Doc Wilkins put on his stethoscope, listened to Myrna's chest. Several long moments passed, with only the sound of Lupe's soft sobbing breaking the silence.

Finally, the doc nodded his head. "Her heart's breathing, but it's very faint. We've got to get them to the clinic right away."

Gregory nodded, reluctantly tearing his eyes away from Angel's face. He went to the buckboard, and worked with the doctor to unroll the collapsible cloth stretchers he kept in the back. First they gathered Myrna's slight body onto one, and placed her in the bed. Then, they returned for Angel and lay her next to her aunt.

As her body touched the surface of the bed, Angel stirred. Her eyes opened, and settled on Gregory's face.

"Gregory," she croaked.

He placed a hand against her scratched and bloodied cheek. "Shh. Don't speak, love. Conserve your strength."

Eyes watery, she asked, "What's happened?"

"We'll talk about it later." He stroked the satin skin, careful of her injuries.

She looked as if she wanted to speak again, but before the words could leave her lips, she lost consciousness again.

Lupe sobbed again, obviously worried about her friend.

Gregory found himself fighting back a tear.

What if he lost her?

What if she never opened those beautiful eyes again?

With her contrary, but passionate ways, she'd worked her way into his heart, and now the thought of losing her was more than he could bear.

Knowing there was nothing more to do except see that she got the necessary medical care, he grasped Lupe's slumped shoulders, and guided her back to the buckboard seat. Then he got on, and the doctor cracked the reins to drive them back toward town, and the clinic.

***

Angel lay on her back, floating on the surface of a body of water. The sun above warmed her face, and she could feel it's heat on her closed eyelids. She could hear the sounds of ducks or mallards, splashing and quacking nearby. She wanted to open her eyes, wanted to take in the scenery she sensed around her, but her heavy eyelids wouldn't obey. They seemed fused in place, and she suddenly felt uneasy, even afraid. She heard the distant sound of Gregory, calling her name, and wanted to reach out, but her arms wouldn't move, either.

She wept; moaning, crying out for him to come and help her.

Then she felt two large, powerful hands on her shoulders. They gently shook her, and the dream fell away as her eyes finally opened.

She blinked a few times, until the face above her came into clear view. When she saw Gregory looking down at her, she burst into tears.

"Oh Gregory, I was so afraid..." the rest of the words she wanted to say disappeared as the sobs overtook her.

He knelt beside her, pulling her into his arms. "It's alright, Angel. I'm here. Everything is alright."

Sitting up proved painful, and she slumped against his strong torso. As if sensing her pain, he released his hold on her, then helped her lie back down.

"Take it easy."

She started to flex her hands, but pain shot up her right arm. Her eyes fell on her wrapped wrist, where the pain had begun, and was now radiating through her upper body, and let her head drop back on the feather pillow beneath her.

She looked around to ascertain her surroundings. The

familiar interior of Doc Wilkins's clinic came into view, and for a moment her foggy mind wondered why she was there. She shifted a bit on the cot, pulled the sheet up around her torso to stave off the chill in the air. But the pains in her arms, neck and shoulders, as well as the burning along her jaw, soon restored her memory. As the events leading to the crash came flooding back to her, her tears began anew. Her whole body shook as she cried, overtaken by a mixture of sadness and anger.

"It's alright, Angel. Doc Wilkins is taking good care of you."

"And Aunt Myrna? Is she..." she let her words fade, unable to finish the question. Her aunt was near seventy years old, and her body wasn't equipped to handle such a catastrophe. Still, she held on to hope, because she didn't want to imagine her life without Aunt Myrna's steadying presence.

He looked somber as he answered her. "She's hanging on, but she's very weak. Doc Wilkins says the next few hours are very critical."

She released a long breath as relief coursed through her. Aunt Myrna might have a rough road ahead, but at least they were both still among the living.

Gregory placed a soft kiss on her forehead, then stood to his full height, towering over her prone form. "I'll fetch the Doc, and he can explain everything to you."

She nodded, offering him a small smile. "Thank you, Gregory."

He smiled back, an affectionate light dancing in his deep brown eyes. "Thank you for not leaving me, love."

And he turned and walked away, his footsteps echoing on the plank floor.

Doc Wilkins appeared above her a few moments later, pulling on a pair of examination gloves. "Afternoon, Miss Lane. It's good to see you're awake. I need to check your injuries."

"How bad is it, Doc?"

He said nothing for a few beats as he lifted the sheet covering her, then reached beneath the thin muslin gown she wore. He palpated her abdomen, and she winced.

"Hmm. You had a gash running across your right hip, but I've stitched it shut. It seems to be starting to heal. That was the worst of it. Everything else was just scrapes and bruises. I've treated them all with some salve."

"So, no broken bones or anything?" She found that hard to believe, considering the soreness than clung to her muscles and joints the way sap clung to a tree trunk.

He shook his head. "No. You did sprain your wrist, and I've wrapped it for you. The soreness you feel is just residual from the impact with the ground. You and your aunt are lucky. The buggy landed in such a way that there was a good amount of space between you two and the solid part of the vehicle. Had it landed on its side the two of you might have been crushed."

She drew a sharp breath. "How is my aunt, Doc? Will she pull through this?"

The doctor looked just as grim as Gregory had earlier. "I can't say for sure yet. She's a fighter, but her injuries are more severe. She has two fractures, one of the a middle rib and one of her left hip, and a shoulder sprain. And I don't have to tell you than her age will make recovery more difficult for her."

She sighed, wishing there was something she could do for her aunt. "I tried to protect her, once I knew the buggy was going to crash."

Doc Wilkins nodded. "We found her lying on top of you. Your maneuver likely saved her life, Miss Lane."

That made her smile. "It's the least I could do. She's been like another mother to me."

The doctor righted her gown and the sheet, then pulled up a stool next to her. "Tell me, do you remember the cause of the crash?"

She nodded, anger flaring inside her. "I sure do. We were

coming home from Aunt Myrna's quilting circle, and some men on horseback gave chase of us. They were firing guns and screaming and carrying on like Sam Hill's own henchmen."

A frown marred the old doctor's face. "Did you tell the deputy this?"

She shook her head.

He rose, stripped off his gloves. "I'm going to get him. He needs to know about these men, so they can be brought to justice."

As he walked away, Angel recalled what little she could about the two men. In the split second she'd been looking backward, just before the buggy crash, she'd seen the face of one of the men in the pale moonlight.

Gregory stalked into the room, his jaw in an angry set. "What's this about night riders terrorizing you?"

She told him the story of what had happened, elaborating on the bit she'd revealed to the doctor a short while ago.

He listened intently, scribbling on a pad of paper with a short pencil. The whole while, his eyes blazed with wrath. "Did you see either one of them well enough to give me a description?"

She nodded. "One of them. I know he was a white man, average build. He had on a bowler hat, and had a dark brown or black beard. Couldn't see his eyes, though."

After he'd taken down the details, he closed the pad and tucked it, along with the pencil, into an inner pocket of his vest. "I'm going to report this to Noah, and we'll set a few of our light horsemen on the trail. Those assholes are not going to get away with this."

From the tight lines of his face, and the violent heat dancing in his eyes, she knew he meant what he said. While she appreciated his determination to avenge her, she did feel a small twinge of guilt. He'd warned her to be cautious around town, and she'd done little but give him guff in return. "I supposed I should have listened to you, about not being out after dark."

He touched his fingertips to her lips. "Don't even mention it, Angel. You, and any other lady of this town, ought to be able to go about your business without fear of being attacked or harassed, day or night. The problem doesn't lie with you. It lies with the cowardly excuses for men who act like such beasts."

"You seem mighty angry, Gregory."

"I am. They had no right to do such a thing. You and Myrna might've been killed, and then what? What in Sam Hill were they thinking of, anyhow?"

She felt the bitterness rise as she remembered the hateful shouts and slurs the men had hurled at her. "They were thinking I was a trouble-making bitch, and that I should leave town."

He stared at her, wide eyed.

"I know that's what they thought, because they shouted as much. I'm no lawman, but I'd bet my saloon they were after me because of my work to win the women of this town the right to vote."

He continued to stare, in stunned silence. Then he stammered a bit. "Why, I never thought..."

She released a sarcastic chuckle. "Oh, come now, Gregory. Don't you see? They're your ilk, these two. How can you be so all-fired mad at what they did, when you once called me a troublemaker yourself? Don't you agree with them?"

He shrank back from her, drawing his hand away. Then he stood, the action so abrupt he sent the stool sliding across the floor. "Now wait just a minute. I don't cotton to ladies being terrorized."

She rolled on her side, turning away from him and his duplicitous ways. "Well you'd best be after them then, Gregory."

He tried again. "Angel, you have to believe me. I might not agree with you but I'd never hurt you over it."

"Just get out, Gregory."

She heard him groan, then listened to his retreating footsteps.

He was offended, and she knew it, but she didn't care. Maybe now he'd see the danger of the bullheaded thinking that so many of the men of this town seemed to be afflicted with. It was a damn shame she and her aunt had almost had to lose their lives to knock some sense into his fool head, but perhaps now he'd change his stance.

A yawn escaped her lips, and she felt the sudden surge of exhaustion take over her body.

Before she could draw her next breath, she was asleep.

Kianna Alexander

Chapter 13

Angel winced as she grasped one of her beer glasses, preparing to put it into the cabinet. The tight gauze wrapping her right wrist did help to stabilize it, but the sprain still hurt whenever she flexed it too much.

"Damn it!" She uttered the curse as the glass slipped from her hand and crashed to the floor, shards scattering across the polished wood.

Lupe rushed over with the broom and dustpan. "Heavens, Angel. That's the third glass today."

Angel rolled her eyes. "I know that, Lupe. I've been keeping count, same as you."

As she stooped to brush the shards onto the dustpan, Lupe shook her head. "Well, one less item in the inventory, I suppose."

Picking up on her friend's disapproving tone, she glared at her. "Lupe, I don't need to be lectured."

"Apparently you do, because if you had any sense at all, you'd stop trying to work so hard. At least give that wrist a few days to heal." Lupe dumped the heap of broken glass into the refuse bin, then replaced the broom and dustpan in the corner where they were kept. Then she leaned against the bar, her hand propped on her hips, as if waiting for her to acquiesce.

Angel sighed. For the last seven years she'd worked at the Crazy Eights, and for the last four, she'd been the proprietor. The old owner, Mr. Greenfield, had gone home to retire with his daughter and grandchildren, and had entrusted her with the care of this place. His confidence meant much to her; she knew how rare it was for a woman of color to own a business. Her own dear mother had never owned so much as a piece of land in the entirety of her lifetime. Her whole heart was in the running of this place, and in making it as successful as possible.

As if she sensed her inner struggle, Lupe rested her hand on her shoulder. " I understand, Angel. I know what the saloon means to you. But you've got to take care of yourself, or you won't have anything left to give."

She knew Lupe was right. Tossing down the towel she'd draped over her shoulder, she blew out a breath, sending the unruly wisps of her hair up and out of her face. "Alright, Lupe. I'll go to the apartment for a nap. We'll just have to allow a bit more time for inventory this month."

Lupe smiled. "Under the circumstances, I think that's very reasonable."

Angel untied her apron and placed it on the shelf beneath the bar counter. Then she trudged down the corridor toward the apartment. Letting herself in with the key, she closed the door behind her.

In the quiet solitude of her apartment, she took a moment to strip off her boots, denims and blouse before crawling into bed, clad in only a thin chemise and her drawers. The last two days had left her exhausted and sore, and she thought sleep would claim her the moment her head touched the feather pillow.

It did not. Instead, she lay there, restless, contemplating all the things that had gone awry as of late.

Aunt Myrna was still at the clinic, convalescing under Doc Wilkins' watchful eyes. Myrna's fever had broken, and she'd come awake for a short while during Angel's visit the previous day. Myrna didn't have any memory of the crash, or how she'd come to be in the clinic, but could clearly remember that night's quilting circle meeting. Angel found relief in that. She didn't want her aunt's recovery hampered by fearful memories. Their chat, while brief, gave her hope that her aunt would rally, and eventually recover fully.

Still, as the doctor reported to her, Myrna still had a long road ahead. She slept day and night, as her frail body struggled to heal from the injuries she'd sustained that horrible night.

Shifting her position so she lay on her side, Angel couldn't help remembering that only a week ago, she and Gregory had been in this very bed, making passionate love. She could clearly recall the feel of his warm, solid body atop hers, the humid kisses he'd given her, and the hot, insistent stroking of his body inside of hers. She let her eyes closed, and she could almost see him there, his bare, muscled chest slick with sweat as he took her. The fantasy sent tingles down her spine, and made liquid heat pool at her core.

She tried to push the memories away, knowing they didn't serve her now. She reminded herself that she would never feel those sensations again, at least not with him. Not after all that had happened.

It was true that Gregory had vehemently denounced the actions of the night riders who'd terrorized them. That denouncement did not negate the fact that he saw her as a troublemaker, and had called her such. Whatever his proclamations now, the fact remained that he believed, just as they did, that women should not be allowed to vote. To her mind, the only difference between Gregory and those two men was the level of action they were willing to take to prove their point.

Tears spilled from her eyes, and she brushed them away angrily. Why should she cry over the likes of him?

She already knew the answer: she loved him. From the day she'd chosen to kiss him instead of slugging him, she'd given him her heart. Now that she knew she could never be with him, her heart was breaking.

Shifting again onto her back, she forced her mind to another matter of far greater importance: the election. Tomorrow would dawn Tuesday, November 6, 1888, and while the town of Ridgeway selected its new mayor, the United States of America would choose her next president. The crash and her subsequent recovery had kept her from spending these last few days on the street, marching and carrying her sign, but her passion for the issues remained the same. She'd kept up with the goings-on by reading the various newspapers Doc Wilkins subscribed to. After her aunt had lapsed back into sleep yesterday, she'd read an article in the *San Francisco Chronicle* about Belva Ann Bennet Lockwood, the only female candidate for president. Mrs. Lockwood had an impressive resume; she was a lawyer, teacher, and an author. Angel doubted men would be impressed by Mrs. Lockwood's list of accomplishments, as she was a woman, and a temperance advocate as well. Under the banner of the National Equal Rights Party, Mrs. Lockwood had already run for the office during the last election of 1884, and apparently intended to have another go at it. Angel respected Mrs. Lockwood's tenacity, and her determination to see her name on the ballot even if no one cast a vote for her.

She stifled a yawn, chuckling to herself at the ridiculousness of it all. If a woman could earn all those diplomas, work hard enough to run for president, and still marry and run a home, why were the men so all-fired determined that women should not vote? It made no sense whatsoever to her, but she knew dwelling on it would only give her a headache.

She yawned again, and let her eyes close as the exhaustion of the past few days finally caught up with her.

***

The curtains covering the windows of the small recovery room at Doc Wilkins's clinic were open, allowing the sun to stream in. Angel sat by her aunt Myrna's bedside, with her copy of *The Canterbury Tales* in her lap. Gregory sat beside her, and his presence did much to comfort her as they watched over the sleeping Myrna in companionable silence.

She was reading The Wife of Bath's Tale, the one her aunt had found so amusing, when Doc Wilkins entered the room.

Kianna Alexander

She and Gregory moved aside, allowing the doctor room enough to get close to Myrna and perform whatever he needed to. Angel watched the doctor check Myrna's pulse, breathing, and temperature, as he'd been doing regularly throughout the day. When he tucked his tools away into his bag, she stopped him.

"How is she doing, Doc?"

Doc Wilkins expression remained pretty even as he answered. "She's a fighter, your aunt. Her temperature is close to normal, and her heart rate's picking up, though it's still a bit slower than I'd like."

"What about her rib? And her hip?"

"The rib will mend itself. But the hip is another matter altogether."

She looked at him intently. "What do you mean?"

"The only way to correct a hip fracture is with surgery. My expertise is a bit more generalized, so I'd have to call on a colleague to perform such a complex procedure, if I thought she could handle it."

She picked up the implications in his words and in his tone, and a shiver went down her back. She knew that whatever the doctor said next, it would not be what she wanted to hear.

The doctor sighed. "There's no easy way to say this, but Myrna is simply too frail to go through major surgery. I've seen cases where people have lived on for years after a hip fracture, without having the corrective procedure. When you combine this with her rib injury, though, things become far more complex. She's presenting symptoms of pneumonia, and I'm not certain her body can fight it off."

The gravity of the doctors words sank into Angel, troubling her. Tears sprang to her eyes as she thought of how her aunt must be suffering. She'd lived more than seventy years, and now she lay there, fighting for her life, all because of some misguided fools who thought terror was the way to get their point across. She pressed her fingertips to her temples, closed her eyes against the pain.

Gregory asked, "Why is she still sleeping so much?"

Doc Wilkins busied himself washing in the basin as he spoke. "I've given her laudanum for her pain. It makes her sleep, but it also keeps her resting so that her body can heal itself as much as possible."

"Thank you." Angel touched the old doctor's hand as he made his way out of the room. Then she and Gregory returned to their seats.

He drew her close to him, letting her recline her head against his shoulder. "Try not to worry, Angel. Maybe she'll rally."

"I dearly hope so." Her aunt was the only living blood relative she had, at least to her knowledge. Beyond that, Myrna was her last link to her mother, and the only one who shared sweet memories of the person her mother had been. Losing that connection might be as great a loss as she'd suffered when her mother died. She didn't want to go through that again; she wasn't entirely sure she could handle it.

"Your aunt is as strong and feisty as any woman I've ever known." Gregory sat in the chair he'd been occupying earlier, and pulled her onto his lap.

Wrapped in the protective circle of his arms, she lay against him and let the tears fall. She wanted to talk, wanted to tell him her fears, but no words would form. All she could manage was few sobs here and there as the fat tears rolled down her cheeks, dampening his shirt front.

He said nothing. His arms tightened a bit around her body, and he held her in silence, letting her release her pain and worry without judgment or interference. After a time the flow of tears slowed, and she calmed a bit, buoyed by his strong, steadying presence. A wave of exhaustion washed over her, and she yawned.

A small sound drew her attention. She turned toward her aunt, just in time to see Myrna's eyes open.

Angel was on her feet and at the bedside in the next moment, with Gregory standing behind her.

Myrna blinked a few times, then her gaze landed on her niece. "Angel May."

She touched her aunt's cheek, felt the heat there. "How do you feel, Aunt?"

Myrna inhaled, winced. The breath rattled around in her chest like grains of rice in a tin can. "Like I was trampled by a herd of buffalo."

"Do you want me to get Doc Wilkins? He can give you some more medicine."

She raised her hand, just a bit, while shaking her gray head."Not yet. That's what's kept me so sleepy, I reckon."

Angel clasped her hand. "But you need your rest, Aunt Myrna. The doctor says it will help you heal."

A soft, wistful smile filled Myrna's face. "Where I'm going, there will be plenty of rest and healing."

She gasped. "Aunt Myrna, don't say..."

Myrna cut her off. "Hush now. Let me talk to you."

Respectfully, Angel nodded.

"I'm old, baby. My body is too weak to fight much longer." She took another breath, this one more shallow, but still labored.

Angel's hand went to her mouth, to cover her sob.

Myrna continued. "Don't cry, child. My life has been a good one, and you have been the best part of it. You're just like my own daughter." She summoned the strength to give her niece's hand a gentle squeeze.

Angel could only nod in response as the tears began to fall anew.

"I love you, Angel May."

"I love you, Aunt Myrna." She leaned down to kiss her wrinkled brow.

Myrna turned her eyes to Gregory. "Well, deputy. Do you think you can take on my niece, and love her real good for me?"

Kianna Alexander

Gregory placed his large hands on Angel's shoulders, giving them an affectionate squeeze as he replied, "I plan to do just that."

The smile on Myrna's face became even more serene. "Good. About time." Her eyelids drooped, but she opened them again.

Angel did her best to compose herself, taking a deep breath.

Myrna winced again, closing her eyes against some unknown discomfort.

Gregory stepped away. "I'll get the doctor."

Left alone with her aunt, Angel felt more helpless that she ever had before. She still clung to her aunt's hand, because she could do nothing else to offer her comfort. The idea of losing Myrna weighed on her as heavily as wool cloak drenched with water. She knew that it would be selfish of her to wish her aunt longer life, if that life was to be marred by pain and loss of independence. So while her aunt lay there, her face tight from whatever was ailing her, she flung a silent prayer heavenward that God would have his way, and that she would have the strength to go on, no matter the outcome.

Gregory returned with the doctor, who already had the vial of laudanum in hand.

Doc Wilkins came to the bedside, and asked, "Myrna, are you in pain?"

Myrna nodded. "My chest. Hurts something fierce."

The doctor extracted a small object from the pocket of his medical coat, wrapped in a handkerchief. He unwrapped it, revealing a spoon. Then he dosed out the medicine, and gave it to Myrna.

She raised her head a bit to accept it, then let her head drop back onto the feather pillow. "Thank you, Doc."

Doc Wilkins offered her a rare, but genuine smile. "Rest easy, now."

Myrna's gaze shifted to Angel and Gregory, standing there

together.

And as she let her eyes slide closed, she said softly, "I will."

Angel stood there, with Gregory behind her, and watched over her sleeping aunt for some time. Finally, as the sun began to dip toward the horizon, she and Gregory left. He escorted her home to her apartment, then left to cover the evening shift at the sheriff's office.

Word came in the wee hours, in the form of Doc Wilkins's nurse, Mary, softly knocking on her door.

Myrna Lane Corcoran had earned her heavenly rest, slipping away peacefully in the night.

Chapter 14

Gregory stood alongside Angel, in his best black suit. His bride-to-be, dressed in the dark gown and veil of a woman in mourning, placed a small bunch of lilies on the freshly turned earth covering her aunt's grave. She knelt there for a few, silent moments, her tears watering the blooms she'd just placed. He stood back, allowing her to grieve in peace.

Lupe, also clad in a dark gown and matching hat, came to kneel beside her friend. Gregory watched as Lupe pulled Angel into her arms, and there on the winter brown grass, rocked her side to side in an attempt to soothe her pain. It touched his heart that Angel had such dear, caring friends, and as he looked around to Lilly, Prissy, Valerie, and the many other women of town who'd come to pay their respects, he knew she'd be alright. They would hold her up; care for her in that certain way women cared for each other, and he would be there to care for her, just as much as she could stand.

In the morning mist, Gregory sat on an old cracker barrel, by the banks of Hibbit's Pond. The small body of water was only a bit removed from the main part of town, and was the closest fishing hole to be found without saddling a horse. He came out here as often as he could manage, most especially when he needed to clear his mind. After the previous day's hardships, he'd known it was time to get his gear. Now, sitting here in the quiet with his line in the water, he felt more at peace than he had in the last several days.

Next to him, Angel May sat on the ground, tending her own line. He hoped that by bringing her out here, she might experience some of the peace he got from fishing. When he'd asked her after the burial, she'd agreed to come along. The two of them had come out before sunrise, and had already caught five fish. The crate between them, lined with pages from old editions of the Tribune, held the morning's catch.

Angel May was the only woman he'd fished with since his mother. He usually fished with Buck, and the two of them could go three hours or more without saying a word to each other. But if she wanted to talk, he would be there to listen to her.

For the moment they sat in convivial silence, each of them focused on the glassy surface of the water.

She spoke, her eyes still on the water. "I miss her, Gregory. I miss her terribly."

His heard the pain in her words, and the love he had for her made him want to take it away. "I know you do, dear."

Her shoulders trembled a bit, and a sob escaped.

He lay down his fishing rod, and left the barrel so he could sit on the ground behind her. She leaned back against him, fat tears falling down her cheeks.

He held her, and let her cry. As much as it hurt him to see her this way, he knew it was only natural. She'd lost the someone she loved dearly, someone who'd anchored her life. She needed to mourn, and he would let her.

Neither of them spoke for a while, he simply let her experience the raw emotions burdening her.

When the sobbing subsided, he gave her a squeeze. "I took your advice, you know."

She sniffled, wiped her face with the back of her hand. "What advice?"

"Remember the day we went to San Francisco? When you told me I should ask my mother if she was happy taking care of us?"

She turned to face him, her brow knit with confusion. "You mean you asked her? How?"

"I wrote her a letter. Got a response from this morning."

She looked intrigued. "What did she say?"

"In brief, she said that she loved us all, and enjoyed taking care of us most of the time. But there were times when we vexed her, she simply didn't show her anger."

She nodded. "I see."

"So it turns out you were right. She wasn't always content with her duties around the house."

A small smile lit her face, and some of the tension left her body. "Well, it is nice to be right now and again."

He squeezed her shoulders, relieved that he could offer her some degree of comfort. She'd been right to question him about his attitudes, and now that he'd heard from his mother, he felt his strict views loosening a bit. Maybe, just maybe, women could play a greater role in society, outside of their households. And maybe if they did, the results wouldn't be as catastrophic as he'd once believed.

He looked down, found her watching him.

"Are you coming around to my side, Gregory?"

He chuckled. "I never said that."

She smiled again, then turned away.

He picked up his pole, but remained seated on the ground with her.

And with her sitting between his open thighs, they refocused their attention on catching more fish.

***

Gregory dusted his hands on his denims. "There. Looks good."

He and Thad had spent the better part of the morning setting up the lobby of Taylor Hotel for today's elections. Gregory had to admit he was somewhat relieved to have finally reached this day. Perhaps after the ballots were cast and this whole election business was completed, things in town would calm down, and some level of peace would be restored. He'd had it with the protests, and the brawls, and the general chaos that surrounded the politics in town.

Kianna Alexander

Thad agreed. "And with time to spare. It's still a little while before folks start coming in."

He checked the old clock above the front desk, and saw that it was seven thirty. The poll didn't officially open until eight, so that gave them a bit of time to relax before the day's work began in earnest.

Thad's voice broke through his thoughts. "How do you think things will turn out today?"

He shrugged. "Who knows? With all the arguing and shouting that's been going on around here lately about women's rights and such, there's really no telling."

Thad ran a hand over his close cropped hair. "You've got a point. Well, Noah's got my vote. Can't say I'm all that fond of Greer."

Standing by the big window that looked out onto Founder's Avenue, he nodded. "Noah's got my vote, too. As far as I'm concerned, Greer's an ass, and not fit to lead a pig to the trough, let alone be mayor of Ridgeway."

That started both men laughing. They were still chuckling when the members of the town council, responsible for working the poll, entered the lobby. Noting the serious looks on the faces of the three old men, Gregory stifled his mirth, and gestured to Thad to do the same.

They watched as the council members set up at the tables, laying out a few pens and inkwells, along with the big book that held the names of the men of town who were authorized to vote. As deputy sheriff, Gregory had a pretty clear understanding of the town's bylaws, and they strictly prohibited any man who was foreign born, owed excessive outstanding debts to a town business, or who had a criminal record from casting a vote. Part of the reason he and Thad were there was to regulate the process. Should a man who'd lost his voting privilege show up and make a fuss, one of the lawmen could haul him in if it became necessary.

From his spot at the window, Gregory could see the early birds of town, out and about to handle the day's business.

Across the street, Henry Carl propped open the door to the livery and blacksmith's shop, while newspaperman McCormack filled the wooden rack outside the newspaper office with copies of today's Ridgeway Tribune. A few folks moved up and down the walk, some headed for the mercantile, or the library.

A gaggle of women came into view as they emerged from the grassy field between the schoolhouse and the rear of the newspaper office and stepped onto the walk. As soon as he saw them, Gregory cursed under his breath. There were ten or so of them, arms linked, and singing something he couldn't identify. The words were muffled by the glass windowpane. What they intended, he had no idea. All he knew was that he wasn't in any mood for foolishness today, and if they created any chaos, he'd have no problem tossing them all into the three empty cells in the sheriff's office.

Seeing their approach made him think of Angel May, though a quick appraisal of their faces told them she wasn't among them. She hadn't spoken to him since the day he'd help take her to the clinic, when she'd compared him to the men who'd attacked her. He knew she was angry, as she had a right to be. What he didn't understand is how she could think of him that way. Had he really been that abrasive with her over the suffrage issue? Did she really think him capable of such base behavior?

He supposed she must think lowly of him, because she'd refused to see him since that day. Whenever they crossed paths on the street, she would go out of her way to avoid him, even crossing the road if necessary. And when he'd shown up at the clinic to visit with Mrs. Corcoran during a time Angel had been present, Doc Wilkins had sent him away, telling him Angel refused to share space with him. He groaned in frustration, running a hand through his hair. How had he come to such an impasse with the woman he cared about? The woman he might even love?

Thad tapped his shoulder, drawing him out of his thoughts

and back to the present. "You alright, Deputy?"

He nodded, trying to convince both his light horseman, and himself. "Yeah, sure, I'm fine."

Looking somewhat unconvinced, Thad jerked his head in the direction of the door. "Gird you loins, sir. The women are coming."

He straightened up, put on a stern face, and prepared for their entrance.

When the women entered, they were silent, having ceased their singing. As he and Thad watched, they fanned out across one wall, each of them taking a seat on the floor with their backs against the striped wallpaper.

The councilmen looked on with interest, as well.

For a few long moments, no one said anything.

Finally, Thad asked, "Alright, ladies. What's the meaning of this?"

The librarian Prissy Parker, who was among the women, spoke up in answer. "It's a sit-in. We're still protesting being denied the vote, just doing so in silence."

Dressmaker Lilly Benigno added, "Yes. So don't worry, we won't interrupt your proceedings."

Gregory quipped sarcastically, "There's a change of pace."

Prissy's brow's knitted angrily, but she held herself in check. "Say what you will, Deputy. We mean to get our point across in a civilized manner." She folded her arms over her chest, directed her eyes straight ahead, and said no more.

Thad turned to him. "Well, we can't put them out, not with them sitting quietly and not raising a fuss."

He shrugged, content with the situation as it was. "No, we can't. But if they're really going to just sit-in, I don't see any harm in it."

Thad nodded, then returned to his post next to the tables where the councilmen sat.

For the first few hours of voting, things remained uneventful. The officers stood at their posts, and the men of town came in, saw the council members for their ballots, cast their votes, and left. The women, true to their word, said nothing, and remained seated, seeming content to watch the proceedings unfold without interfering. A sense of calm settled over Gregory, and he began to think that this day might go by without incident.

The door swung open, and he turned his head to see who was coming in.

His chest tightened immediately at the sight.

There, framed by the open doors, stood his beautiful Angel May. With the sunlight streaming in around her, she looked every bit as radiant an ethereal as her name suggested. A snow white, long sleeved blouse covered her upper body, while a pair of snug fitting denims clung to her hips like a second layer of skin. Her injured wrist was still wrapped.

Her sparkling bronze eyes met his, but they held no expression. They were as cool as the air in an icebox.

The barmaid Lupe accompanied her as she moved into the space, and he noticed the slight limp punctuation her gait. She was obviously still sore, and still angry with him, because she was making a show of ignoring him. She stooped low, grimacing a bit as she did, as she stopped to greet each and every one of the women who'd posted themselves up against the wall for the so-called 'sit-in.' That done, she moved to the end of the line, next to the schoolteacher Janice Smart. Lupe fetched her a chair, to keep her from having to sit on the floor, and Angel sat.

He watched the women for a few moments, noting the way Angel avoided looking in his general direction. They were carrying on a hushed conversation about something; he couldn't make out what they were saying, and he didn't much care. What he did care about was Angel, and making her talk to him, despite her obvious determination to the contrary.

So he left his post by the booths and strode across the room to where she sat.

Kianna Alexander

***

Angel was well aware of Gregory standing over her. There was no denying his presence, due to his massive size, and the heady aroma of pine and cigar tobacco that seemed to swirl around him like an aura. She could sense his annoyance as he stood there, waiting for her to acknowledge him. But she was speaking to Janice, and she refused to stop herself mid-sentence just because he'd lumbered over to stare down at her.

He cleared his throat loudly; she ignored him. She felt no need to jump at his every whim.

When she'd said her piece to the schoolmarm, she looked up at him. He stood there glaring at her, his big arms folded over his chest. For all the world, she thought he looked like an angry bear who'd just had a fat salmon escape his grasp. Keeping her face impassive, she said, "Hello."

He cocked a thick eyebrow. "What are you doing here?"

She responded with a slight shrug. "Why shouldn't I be here?"

He frowned for a moment before speaking again. "You should be home, resting. You've been through a lot."

She gave a nonchalant chuckle, completely free of humor. "You're not in any position to tell me what to do."

That seemed to rile him. His nostrils flared, his eyes flashed with anger. "Angel May, this isn't a time for being stubborn and petty. I'm only thinking of your welfare."

She scoffed. Stubborn and petty indeed. He was the one who's opinions were so unchangeable, it was if they were cast in stone. "Honestly, Gregory. I'm an adult, and I'm perfectly capable of..."

The rest of her words slipped back down her throat unspoken as he grabbed her around the waist, lifting her from her seat. In the next breath, he draped her over his shoulder like a buffalo pelt, and started striding.

Gasps and exclamations of shock rose from the assembled women.

She balled her good hand into a fist, beat against his shoulder. "Put me down!"

He ignored her as he approached Thad.

Gruffly, he asked, "Thad, can you handle things here for a while?"

An amused Thad laughed as he bobbed his head. "Sure."

Angel did not share the young man's amusement, and she struggled against Gregory's grasp as he turned and carried her toward the door. The bruising she'd taken in the buggy crash had not yet healed completely, and the more she twisted against him, the more the dull pain intensified. As he kicked open the door, she gave up the ghost and let him carry her out, lest the pains morph into full-on throbbing misery.

Outside, she cast her angry eyes on the townsfolk moving up and down the walk, all of whom seemed interested enough in her plight to stare, yet didn't bother to intervene. Folks merely stepped aside and Gregory toted her up the walk, heading north up Town Road, toward the picnic shelter in the grassy field.

When they arrived there, he sat her down, her hips coming to rest atop one of the wooden picnic tables beneath the shelter. Now she took on his former stance, folding her arms over her chest and letting her face crease into a rather unpleasant frown.

Since the crash, and the subsequent loss of her aunt, she'd been a ball of emotions. Angry one moment, sad the next; cycling between crying and laughing. Right now, though, everything about his manner seemed infuriating, and she meant to tell him all about it.

He stood there, hands shoved in his pockets, staring at her intently.

When she realized he wasn't speaking, she lay into him.

Her index finger extended in his direction, she shouted, "Have you got sawdust where your brains ought to be? What in the hell do you mean by picking me up and toting me through town like that?"

His eyes tracked the movements of her wagging finger for a few moments, before he reached out and pushed her hand down. "Holster that damn finger, Angel May, and listen to me."

"I'll do no such thing. You're a simpleton of the highest order if you think I'm interested in anything you have to say, after what you did. You're lucky I haven't slugged you right in your fool mouth!" She made a move to slide off the table top, so she could get away from his foolery, and go back to the sit-in where she belonged.

He moved closer, his big body blocking her path of exit. His powerful thighs pressed against her knees where they dangled over the side of the table, effectively immobilizing her.

His dark eyes beneath the brim of his Stetson bored into hers, and she could see the urgency in his gaze.

"You know, the last time you threatened to slug me, you kissed me instead."

She closed her eyes against his intense gaze, and against the memory of that kiss. That was the day he'd ceased being just the deputy to her, the day he'd come to mean so much more. The moment their lips touched, her heart had escaped its gilded cage and landed in his possession.

"So you remember that," she heard him say.

She took a deep breath, opened her eyes again. "Don't toy with me, Gregory. I'm not some empty-headed doxy, and as long as you keep up your foolish, male superior way of thinking, I can't be with you. I won't."

His gaze never wavered, and when he spoke again, his tone was serious. "What if I told you I've changed my mind?"

"I wouldn't believe you." She stated the fact as clearly as it existed in her own mind.

Kianna Alexander

He wasn't deterred. "You don't have to believe it, but I really have changed my mind. Before, I was sure women ought to keep to their cooking and cleaning and child-raising. Now, I see things differently."

She rolled her eyes. Was this just an attempt to get back in her good graces? "Oh, and just what caused you to have this miraculous epiphany, after a whole lifetime of wrong-headed thinking?"

Something in his gaze changed, and she saw a level of sincerity in his eyes she'd never seen before. "You were right about my mother. Maybe you're right about this as well. All I know is I don't want to fight you on this anymore."

She blinked, watching him intently.

"Listening to you describe the moments leading up to the buggy crash. When I heard you talk about those men, and what they shouted at you, I was taken back to the moment we found you and Myrna underneath that buggy..." his words trailed off, as if he were leaving something unsaid. His head drooped, and she sensed the sadness hanging over him.

She crooked her finger, placed it under his chin to prompt him to look at her.

When their eyes connected, he continued. "You were so still, and barely breathing. I realized that I could have lost you. You could have been taken from me, all because of this suffrage issue. After what I saw that day, I don't care to fight progress anymore. I'm not going to lose you, Angel May. Not now, and not ever."

His words, dripping with affection and sincerity, touched her very soul. The flaring anger she'd felt when he tossed her over his shoulder was doused, like a fire drowned out by a torrent of water. She let her fingertips graze over the hard line of his jaw. "Gregory."

His expression softened as she spoke his name, and he mimicked the touch, stroking a finger along her jaw.

"Forgive me, Angel May. I love you."

Hearing the sweet endearment from his mouth made her heart soar. "Truly?"

"Madly."

She felt the smile spread across her face, and across her very being. "That's a relief, because I love you, too."

He said nothing more, and leaned in.

His lips crushed against hers, and the world fell away as she reacquainted herself with the feel and taste of him. His mouth was as warm and inviting as she remembered, and the faintest notes of coffee hung on his tongue as it stroked and danced against hers. Her arms wound around his neck as he wrapped his around her waist, pulling their bodies as close together as their positioning would allow. Without breaking the kiss, she parted her legs and slid her hips to the very edge of the table, allowing their bodies to come in even closer contact.

He groaned against her mouth as the hard evidence of his desire pressed against her lower belly.

The sound of someone giggling invaded her mind, and she reluctantly broke the seal of their lips to turn toward the sound.

There, a few feet from the shelter, stood a grinning Lupe. "Carry on. I'll go and tell the girls that you and the deputy are back on good terms." She winked before turning and heading back down the walk toward the hotel.

Heat rushed to Angel's face, her cheeks burning with embarrassment. "Wonderful. Before we get make it back to the hotel, folks will be setting a wedding date for us."

He responded with a broad smile. "You're probably right, so why don't we set one for ourselves?"

She hugged him then, rested her head on his strong shoulder, unable to wipe the giddy smile from her face. "That's the best offer I've had all day."

Kianna Alexander

Chapter 15

Gregory reluctantly released his hold on Angel's hand as they stepped inside the confines of the Taylor Hotel. Their entrance drew a wave a of applause from the women still seated on the floor along the wall, and a few hoots from the men who'd come to cast their ballots. He smiled, enjoying the way Angel's face flushed with redness at the attention. He returned to his post, watching as she returned to her seat among her cohorts.

Thad eased over, wearing a broad grin. "Looks like the two of you are on pretty good terms, eh?"

Gregory leaned his back against the wall. "I'm sure Lupe told you as much. What about you and our schoolmarm?"

Thad's eyes grew as big as two full moons for a moment, then he coughed. "What are you talking about?"

He gave the young officer a playful slap on the back. "You've been staring at her all day, Thad. I'm sure other folks have noticed it, too."

Thad cleared his throat, his gaze trained on Miss Smart. "I..uh...I'm going back to my post."

He watched with knowing eyes as Thad retreated across the room to his appointed post. He chuckled to himself, knowing how useless it was to try and fight an attraction to a woman, but decided to let young Thaddeus Stern learn that lesson in his own time.

The lunch hour passed, and Gregory checked his pocket watch. His rumbling stomach demanded food, and luckily, Mrs. Taylor came around again, this time bearing ham sandwiches, Saratoga chips, and lemonade for he and Thad. The women, resourceful as always, had brought in their own lunches, and were now eating and chatting.

As he sat down in one of the vacant chairs to eat, he kept a watchful eye on Angel. She was engrossed in conversation with Lupe and Janice Smart, who were sitting on either side of her. Every now and then, though, she'd cast a glance in his direction, fluttering those lush, dark lashes whenever their gazes met. He took a long swig of lemonade, both to wash down his food, and to cool the rising heat of desire he felt for his sweet Angel. He couldn't wait for the day to end, so he could secret her away to some quiet place and show her just how much he'd come to love her.

Once their meals were eaten and cleared away, he and Thad returned to their posts to watch over the last few hours of voting. Town law dictated that all men of town be allowed a half day off on Election Day, either in the morning or afternoon, as dictated by the employer. The polls would close promptly at three pm., so that votes could be tallied and a result announced by seven. At a little after one, Noah came in with his wife, Valerie on his arm. The two of them greeted the women, as well as the other voters assembled there, with warm greetings and smiles. Then, without much fanfare, Noah cast his vote, and he and his wife departed. Gregory tipped his hat to his friend and boss, and wished him luck as he and Mrs. Rogers slipped out.

As the two o'clock hour drew near, the doors of the hotel swung open, and Nathan Greer and his contingent sauntered in. Nathan, dressed in a fancy but ill-fitting suit, marched over to the table to check in, without so much as a glance in the direction of the women. As he passed Gregory, he gave him a crooked, insincere smile. Gregory merely nodded to him, and the two other men who followed behind him as if they were being led about on invisible leashes. He would have been content to ignore Nathan and his lackeys; however, his lawman's instinct told him to be wary.

Keeping his demeanor calm and his face impassive, he watched the two men, discreetly sizing them up. Both were dressed in all black, a stark contrast to Nathan Greer's too tight, too bright suit in a gaudy shade of green. Though they'd shown up with Greer at the polls, neither of them registered with the councilmen; it seemed they hadn't come to vote, but were merely accompanying Greer. He also noticed both men were wearing their hat brims so low, and their collars so high, that it was hard to see their faces. One wore a red kerchief around his neck, pulled up over his chin. If he were a man to bet, he'd put his money on the two of them being trouble. In his experience, no blameless man went through so much trouble to conceal his identity.

He swung his gaze to Thad, and gave a small jerk of his head to signal him. Thad touched his hat brim, indicating that he understood.

As Greer emerged from behind the curtain of one of the booths, he cast a disapproving eye on the assembled women, as if he were just now noticing their presence.

Greer bellowed, "Come now, ladies. You've no business here, since you're not allowed to vote. Don't you have some washing or cooking you should be doing? Should your husbands have to go without a hot meal or a clean shirt, just so you can make trouble?"

Prissy Parker fired back, "Oh, go sit on a tack, Greer."

Lilly Benigno added, "Yes, do. It might improve your disposition."

Greer's brow furrowed, but he said nothing else. He made his way to the door, his chest puffed out so far he looked like a perturbed ape. The two men with him trotted along behind him, so closely that one of them bumped into him.

Greer grunted as he pushed the man back. "Not so close!"

As the man stumbled a few steps, his hat fell off of his head, revealing some of his features; shaggy, dark brown hair and brown eyes came into view. He bent to grab up his hat.

Before he could replace it, Angel cried out. "You!" She stood to her feet, pointing her finger at the man.

The dark haired stranger's jaw twitched as he replaced his hat. He muttered, "I don't know what you're talking about, lady."

Angel, her eyes now filling with tears, turned her gaze to Gregory. "That's him! The one who chased us!"

Gregory felt hot, blinding anger rising in him like lava ascending to the top of a volcano. In the next second, he'd crossed the room and grabbed the man by his collar. Thad, ever the watchful officer, eased behind the other man and restrained his arms behind his back.

Greer, as if angry to have his hangers-on detained, drew up in a show of offense. "What's the meaning of this? Why are you accosting my friends?"

Gregory sneered at him. "Your illustrious friends are wanted on charges of harassment and murder." The man he held by the collar struggled against him, trying to free himself. His friend in the red kerchief seemed a bit more level-headed, and made no move to get away from Thad.

Twisting and squirming, he cried, "I ain't done nothin'!"

Angel, now being supported by Janice and Lupe, appeared visibly shaken and distraught. "You've done nothing but kill my aunt, you piece of shit. I'll never forget your hideous face so long as I live."

The man's eyes widened, and he fought a little harder to get away from Gregory's grasp.

"Enough of this." Gregory snatched the mans arm's behind his back, fitting him with the iron bracelets from his gun belt.

"Aw, come on! She's lyin'!" The man groused as the cuffs closed around his wrists.

That made Gregory's dander rise, but he held himself in check. He didn't want the ladies present to witness him whipping this man's ass until the blood poured from his nose. "Don't slander her any further. You're under arrest, and if you say another word, I'll knock your teeth so far down your throat you'll be walking on them. Understand?"

The man said no more, but his jaw remained tight.

Greer, as if coming to his senses, asked the man, "Jimmy.

Did you really do this?"

Jimmy gave only a shrug. "You was always talking about how the women was makin' trouble for you. Me and Bobby thought we'd scare 'em, you know, maybe make 'em keep quiet."

For the first time, Nathan Greer seemed speechless. In the ensuing silence, the women all stood to their feet, leveling the three men with a variety of scolding and downright vicious stares. Angel dabbed her eyes, but composed herself to join in.

Eyes blazing, Angel said, "You succeeded in scaring us, but we won't be put off. Right is right. You'll both rot in hell for what you've taken from me."

Thad announced, "Open the doors, Greer. Your boys are going to the lockup."

Still wide-eyed and silent, Greer did as he was told, holding open the door.

Gregory kicked Jimmy in the back of his shin. "Get moving, you dolt."

The five of them left the hotel, and moved down the walk toward the sheriff's office. There, Jimmy and Bobby were each shoved into a cell and locked in, while Nathan Greer sat by the desk, vehemently denying any knowledge of what his boys had done.

Greer seemed uncharacteristically nervous, even embarrassed, as he rambled on. "Honestly, sheriff, I wouldn't send those boys to do such a fool thing. And if I'd known, do you think I'd have brought them to polls with me?"

Gregory considered that. Even Greer had to be a little bit smarter than to bring two known criminals out in public with him. "I see your point. What do you think, Thad?"

Thad, standing by the door with his arms folded over his chest, said, "Man would have to be pretty stupid to bring 'em, if he knew they were guilty."

Gregory shifted his gaze back to Greer. "Alright then. I

won't put you in the lockup, for now. But don't go trying to skip town, you may be called on to testify. Got it?"

Greer nodded, then stood. "I got it." He turned to leave, only to be stopped in the doorway by his wife, Persephone.

Eyes filled with tears, Persephone said, "Nathan, I've just come from the hotel. How could you be involved in such things?"

Greer's manner changed, softening considerably. "Perry, my love. I wasn't involved. You must believe me!"

She dashed away a fallen tear. "How can I?"

Gregory felt a pang of sympathy for the man, though he couldn't guess why. "Mrs. Greer, we're not arresting your husband, because we believe his story. There's no indication he was involved."

That seemed to calm her, but she still looked a bit sad. She nodded to them, then turned and walked away, with her husband following close behind her.

Gregory stood in their wake. "Thad, I'm going back to mind the polls until they close. You stay here with these two maggots."

Thad slid into the chair behind the desk. "Sure thing. You know, if you wanted to get a few good licks in on them, I'd look the other way."

Gregory shook his head, adjusting his hat as he stood in the open door. "Why do you think I'm leaving you here with them, instead of staying? I'll see you later."

By the time he returned to the hotel, it was a quarter till three. The whole lobby was abuzz with chatter. He immediately went to Angel's side.

"Are you alright, Angel May?"

She gifted him with a small smile. "I'm much better now that those two are off the streets."

He squeezed her shoulders, then placed a soft kiss on her brow. "Good."

And he returned to his post, to watch over what remained of the voting, and his lady love.

***

As the four o'clock hour came on, Angel unlocked the rear door to her apartment and opened it. Slipping inside, she waited for Gregory to enter before closing it behind her.

She stepped out of her flat slippers, and took off her wrap. She hung them on the coat rack with Gregory's hat and vest, then turned to him. He stood there, a ghost of a smile on his handsome face, watching her.

"It's been a crazy day." The deep timbre of his voice filled the silence.

"It has." She stepped into his space, wound her arms around his neck. "And I'd like nothing more than for you to make me forget it all."

He groaned as he lowered his head, his lips touching hers. The kiss was soft at first, but quickly became more urgent, more filled with need. Her lips parted, allowing his tongue into the cavern of her mouth. He grasped her around the waist, pulling her body close until it was flush with his. His manhood pressed against her belly, as hard as a length of iron, and she felt the shiver of desire spark there and spread through her whole body.

He finally broke the kiss, his hands going to the pearl buttons running down the front of her white blouse. He fumbled with them a bit, popping off a couple of the buttons, until he finally opened the garment. Reaching into the top of her lacy chemise, he lifted out one of her breasts and worked his thumb over the dark nipple. Her head fell back, and she sighed with pleasure.

"Have I ever told you how glad I am that you don't wear corsets?"

She was too busy panting to speak, so she shook her head.

"Then let me show you." And he dipped his head, drawing the pert nipple into his mouth.

Her knees buckled, but his strong arm around her waist

braced her, providing the stability her legs could not. He remained there, suckling her with ardor, until her legs felt no stronger than than two blades of grass swaying in a harsh wind.

Mercifully he stopped, and as she fought to catch her breath, he lifted her into his arms again. This time, she put up no resistance whatsoever as he carried her through the open doorway into her bedroom, placing her gently atop the quilts.

There, he took his own sweet time stripping the remaining clothing from her body, while placing soft kisses on each bit of flesh he bared. When she was nude, he stood, his eyes smoldering as he undressed himself. "When shall we marry, my love?"

Lying there, pulsing and trembling, she composed herself as best she could before answering him. "Whenever you please."

He smiled then, kicking away the pile of clothes he'd stripped off.

Her eyes strayed to the part of him that her body ached for. He was erect and beautiful, and she could hardly wait to take him inside. *My, he's wonderfully made.*

"That's a very good answer. Let me reward you.." He joined her on the bed, the mattress giving a bit beneath their combined weight.

He rolled her over onto her back, positioning himself between her open thighs. In the next moment, he slid inside her, and she welcomed him into the place she most wanted him to be. Their eyes locked, and she felt as if their very souls were touching, embracing. She wrapped her legs around his waist, and as his hand cupped her bottom and his thrusts increased in pace and depth, nothing else mattered but the two of them, and the magical ecstasy created by the joining of their bodies.

Later, beneath the rumpled bedclothes, Angel started from a comfortable sleep by the sound of someone pounding on her door, the one in the corridor leading to the saloon up front. She slid from beneath Gregory's embracing arm, leaving him to his slumber. After she'd put on a dressing gown and robe, she went to the door to see what was amiss. She checked the peephole, and seeing Lupe there, swung the door open.

"What is it?"

Lupe, grinning from ear to ear, chided, "My, my. You're in bed awful early, Angel."

Rolling her eyes at her friend's teasing, she repeated her original question. "What is it, Lupe?"

She paused a minute, as if she'd forgotten why she'd come. Then, she said, "The election results are in, and Noah won!"

Angel clapped her hands together. "That's wonderful! Any news of the presidential race yet?"

"Not yet. We should know something soon. Lilly Benigno and Prissy Parker are waiting down at the telegraph office for the wire to come in."

Angel smiled, genuinely happy for Noah. She liked him, approved of his views, and thought he would make an excellent mayor of Ridgeway. "Well, this is good news. I'm supposing that also means my Gregory is going to be sheriff now."

"Your Gregory, eh?" Lupe ribbed her gently with her elbow.

"Oh, go on, Lupe. No use trying to hide it now."

"You're right about that. Well, I'll let you get back to your...bed."

With a giggle, Lupe traipsed down the corridor, and disappeared back into the saloon. For a brief moment, Angel could hear the revelry going on in the saloon; it seemed she wasn't the only one pleased with Noah's victory. After Lupe closed and locked the door up front, Angel did the same to her door, and eased back into bed with Gregory.

He rolled over to face her as she slipped beneath the

covers. "What's going on, love?"

"Looks like Noah's won the election."

A broad grin filled his handsome face. "Hot damn! I'm gonna be sheriff."

"I'm very happy for you, honey." His excitement was obvious, and a bit contagious. She placed a celebratory kiss on his cheek.

"Good. Then you'll have no problem helping me out."

Confusion knit her brow. "What do you mean?"

"Well, now that I'm sheriff, I want to make a few changes to the police force."

"Like what?"

He touched her cheek. "Like making you Ridgeway's first female peace officer."

Shock made her breath release in a whoosh. "What?"

"You heard me. I want you to be one of my peace officers."

She let his words penetrate her mind for a moment. A peace officer? She'd never considered such a line of work, but that didn't mean she couldn't see the enormity of his offer. She searched his face, looking for any hint that he might be making a joke. Only sincerity met her. "You're serious, aren't you?"

He nodded. "I am."

She thought about his words a few weeks ago, about a woman's natural place. She remembered the times he'd spouted such male superior nonsense that she'd wanted to box his ears. Still, looking at him now, she sensed a change in him. It was a total shift in his beliefs, and up until this very moment, she'd thought it impossible he'd ever reach this place of enlightenment.

"I feel I'm making a solid decision here. I mean, I've seen with my own two eyes that you can handle yourself- you nearly knocked out that fellow who touched your behind. You're smart, resourceful, and damn near fearless. Those are the qualities that make a good law officer, and I'd be honored if you'd wear the uniform alongside me and the others."

She could only shake her head in amazement as she contemplated his words. "Heavens."

"Hell, you've got such a mean hook, you may not even need a sidearm."

Peals of laughter rolled out of her mouth at that, and he chuckled right along with her, his arm draped easily over her side.

When the laughter subsided, and she looked into his eyes again. "I believe you're serious, and I really appreciate the offer. But I already have a job. The Crazy Eights is my place, and that's where I belong."

He pursed his lips, looked thoughtful. "I hadn't really thought about it, but I guess I would be taking you away from your business if I hired you on."

"So you understand why I can't be a peace officer, then?"

He bobbed his head affirmatively. "Yep. But I'm still gonna be looking to hire a few female officers, and I'd like your help with that, if you don't mind."

She smiled. "I can do that."

"Now, there's one more thing I want to know."

Grazing her fingertips over his jaw, she said, "What?"

"How do you feel about getting married on Christmas Eve?"

Happy tears sprang to her eyes. This was a day she'd never forget. She'd protested at the polls, been carried through town, and gotten a job offer and a marriage proposal. And it was all because of the man lying next to her, whose presence warmed her, body and soul.

Gazing into his eyes, she smiled. "Let's do it."

Chapter 16

As Thanksgiving came and went, November fading into December, he kept watch over his sweet Angel May. The saloon was closed, and not set to reopen until after the new year, so that she could have the time she needed to grieve. By the end of the first week of December, he could see her beginning to rally. She smiled more readily, even laughed a bit, and begun to talk with her friends about wedding plans. While his body yearned for her, he put off his needs in favor of hers. With their nuptials approaching, and given the recent tragedy she'd experienced, he decided not to press her. He'd wait until their wedding night to make love to her again, and he would make sure it was a night she'd never forget.

More than anything, he wanted to restore her to full happiness, and he had in mind a very special wedding gift. His mind set, he made an appointment to visit Emerson Construction.

Easing his chair up to the round wooden table, Gregory watched Rod Emerson spread out a large sheet of butcher's paper over the surface. Rod, the town's main builder, was responsible for the construction of most of the newer buildings in town, including the Doris Ridgeway Primary School, the Taylor Hotel, and Ruby's Restaurant. A graphite pencil tucked behind his ear, Rod took a seat across from Gregory.

"So, Deputy. Tell me what your vision is for your home."

That drew a shrug from Gregory. "The first thing I'll need is a good piece of land."

Rod looked thoughtful. "I've got about seven available plots between here and Oakland. Will you be farming?"

"I don't think so. Angel might want a flower bed, or an

herb garden, but not much more."

"Smallest plot I have is just under two acres. I think it's suit you nicely, based on what you're telling me."

Gregory nodded. "Sounds like plenty."

Rod took the pencil from behind his ear, poising it over the butcher paper. "One story or two? And how many bedrooms?"

He scratched his head as he thought on the question. He supposed he could have asked Angel for her input on the house they would one day live in, but he's wanted to keep the visit a surprise. He had a very special way of telling her about the house in mind. "One story, and let's say three bedrooms. That's one for us, one for my parents when they visit, and one for a babe."

Rod's face showed a smile as he sketched on the butcher paper, drawing a single large rectangle. Then he began to make several straight lines and angles within the rectangle, to represent the walls of the house. Gregory watched as he drew in more details, such as the windows and doors, admiring Rod's skill with the pencil.

When Rod started to add on to the drawing, beyond what Gregory had asked for, he stayed the architect's drawing hand.

"Hold on, now. That might be a bit more than we can afford."

Rod waved him off as he continued to draw. "Pshaw. Tell you what. I'll add on the sitting porches on the front and back, and a fourth bedroom, no charge. What you're asking for is pretty modest, you know."

Gregory stared. "Are you serious? You'd do that for us?"

Rod nodded. "O'Course! After what Angel May's been through, she deserves every bit of happiness she can get. Call it my wedding gift to the two of you."

"Thank you. Thank you very much." Gregory watched as Rod continued his work. When the drawing was finished, he was truly in awe of the plans. The home he would live in with Angel, where they would raise their children, was going to be a grand home indeed.

Rod extended his hand, and Gregory took it, giving it a hearty shake.

Gregory knew how much he would be making as sheriff, and the raise would do much toward paying for the house and the parcel of land it would be built on. He'd lived a relatively simple existence, and had managed to put away a tidy sum of money in an account at Ridgeway Bank and Telegraph. "How much will I need to pay today, and what are the terms?"

Rod extracted a stack of papers from a small side table, and set them between him. He went over the cost of the house and land together, and they came to an agreement on the terms. Since the full amount was only a few hundred dollars more than Gregory had saved, Rod agreed to take as much as he could pay, then take the rest in two equal payments, due by March, when construction should be complete. Once Gregory had written the bank draft, and received a copy of the plans and contracts, he said his goodbyes to Rod, and stepped outside.

He'd only made it a few steps down the walk before he heard someone calling his name.

Turning his head, he saw Daisy Trice, the young telegraph clerk and bank assistant, coming down the walk toward him.

"Deputy, you received a reply to your wire a few days ago. I didn't want to trouble you, what with the funeral and all, but here it is."

He took the offered slip from Daisy's hand. "Thank you, Miss Trice."

She gave him a smile and a nod, then headed back toward the building housing the bank and telegraph office.

He lifted the slip up, reading the words printed on it. It was from his father, Nigel.

Good news, indeed! Expect us in mid-December. Your mother,

Luke, and I will remain in Ridgeway with you until after the new year, to see you married and installed as sheriff. Love, Pa.

The news brought a smile to his face. He'd not seen his family in over eighteen months, since he'd gone to visit them when his nephew, Jack Jr., had celebrated his first birthday. Now, not only would he get to see them again, but he'd get to introduce them to his sweet Angel May, so they could see how wonderful she was.

He tucked the slip into the pocket of his denims, and set his feet toward Angel's apartment, to tell her of their arrival.

When she opened the door, he leaned down to greet her with a kiss, before stepping inside.

She shut the door behind him. "You look chipper."

He pulled the telegraph slip from his pocket and handed it to her.

She walked to the settee while reading it, and he followed her. By the time they were both seated she'd finished.

Her next question caught him by surprise. "Do they know I'm colored?"

He nodded. "Yes, I told them. What made you ask that?"

"I never met them before, and not everyone is as open minded as you, Gregory."

He supposed he should have considered that. "Ridgeway's a pretty progressive town, but even a few of the older folks around here aren't too pleased about it."

She said nothing, but her expression belied her worries.

"Don't worry. My sister-in-law is mulatto, so we've already dealt with this kind of thing."

She eyed him curiously. "Really. And how did that go over with your folks?"

He laced his fingers together in his lap. "I'll admit they were a bit apprehensive at first. Once they met Anna and discovered how sweet she was, and how much she loved Jack, they took to her just fine."

She leaned closer to him, and he slipped his arm around

her shoulders.

Eventually she spoke again. "So what you saying is as long as I charm them, and they know I love you, we won't have any problems?"

"That's right."

That seemed to reassure her, because she smiled as she snuggled closer to him.

He held her close, thinking of the plans for their home nestled inside his vest. The future held so much promise for the two of them, he could hardly wait to see where their love would take them.

***

Angel stood by the mirror over her dresser, surveying her reflection one last time. At any moment, Gregory's parents and his younger brother would arrive at the saloon for Sunday dinner. Only a week remained until the Christmas holiday, and less than that until she and Gregory's Christmas Eve wedding. Between the last minute planning for the ceremony and reception, and the cooking and cleaning for today's family meal, she'd barely had time to dress. The business of the day had sapped a great deal of her energy, but she'd put on her best teal colored gown anyhow, prepared to soldier on into the evening.

Gregory appeared behind her, wrapping his arms around her waist. "You look lovely, dearest. Don't fret over it."

She turned to face him, placing a hand against his bearded jaw. "You look very handsome as well, Gregory." And he did. Her appreciative eyes drank in the sight of him in the deep blue suit and snow white shirt draped over his muscled frame.

"Thank you. Let's hope my mother agrees. Otherwise she will task you with dressing me for the rest of my life." He winked.

She shook her head. "Silly goose. Let's go up front and make sure everything is ready."

They walked, hand in hand, into the saloon. The largest of the round tables had been put in the center of the floor, to accommodate the family gathering. Lupe and Valerie had been by earlier to help out, and had set a lovely table, complete with a snow white tablecloth, gleaming silver, cut crystal glasses, and china dishes hand painted with delicate pink rosebuds. A vase filled with colorful wildflowers centered it all.

She smiled as she took in the sight. "The next time I see Lupe I shall kiss her. I couldn't wish for a dearer friend."

Gregory looked impressed as well. "It does look nice."

The two of them set about arranging the food, which was in a polished silver service, in the center of the table around the flower arrangement. A chilled pitcher of lemonade soon joined the food.

Angel had just set the glass dish holding her lemon tart down when she heard a voice behind her, calling her intended's name.

She turned to see Gregory's family standing by the propped open door.

Gregory clasped her hand, and led her to where his family stood.

Angel smiled, offering her greetings to Gregory's father, mother, and younger brother. She'd met them briefly three days ago, when they'd first arrived in town. Tired from their long journey by train and stagecoach, they'd been eager to check into their room at the Taylor Hotel. Tonight, she hoped to get to know them a bit better.

Gregory's father Nigel, kissed her hand. "Angel. A delight to see you again." Nigel's coloring was bit darker than Gregory's. He was tall and lean in stature, and his short, gray hair was speckled with white. Wire rimmed spectacles sat on the end of his nose.

She smiled, but before she could speak a reply, Gregory's mother Marie swept her into a tight hug. "Hello again, my dear."

Angel returned the embrace. She already liked Marie, whose kindness more than compensated for her short stature. Marie's salt and pepper hair was swept into a chignon, and she wore a lovely blush colored gown over her plump frame.

The ever gallant Luke, Gregory's younger brother, stepped forward. He wore a blue shirt beneath his dark suit, and wore his long dark hair back in a low ponytail. He was very handsome, and she wondered if the young women in Sacramento might be stricken with love sickness at the sight of him.

Luke mimicked Nigel's gesture by kissing her hand. "You look lovely."

"Thank you, Luke." Angel stepped back to allow them entry into the saloon.

Everyone came in, and took seats around the table.

Marie commented,"You've set a lovely table, dear, and I can't wait to see what we're having."

"Whatever it is, it smells wonderful." Nigel opened his napkin and spread it over his lap.

Smiling at the people who would soon become her family, Angel stood and began lifting the lids off the dishes she and Gregory had prepared. Soon she'd revealed the spread: a glazed ham dotted with cloves, seasoned diced turnips, fried potatoes, early peas with pearl onions, and her lemon tart for dessert.

Every man at the table stood along with her.

She felt the blush filling her cheeks at their show of chivalry. "Sit down, you all. I'm just serving."

Nigel and his two sons did as she requested.

Luke whistled. "Brother, if she feeds you like this everyday, you'll soon be as fat as Uncle Franklin."

Gregory ribbed his brother. "Stuff it, Luke. You're just jealous."

Watching the two of them tease each other made Angel chuckle. She loved the way they went at each other; it was easy to see they cared for one another. She began to dole out servings of the food onto the china plates, taking her seat again when everyone was served.

Nigel led them in a brief prayer, then they dug into the offerings.

Taking a sip of the tart lemonade, Angel asked, "When will I have the chance to meet Jack?"

Marie answered that. "He's home with his wife Anna. She's due to have our second grandchild any time now, so he couldn't travel."

Hearing the delight in Marie's voice as she mentioned her coming grandchild made Angel think of her future with Gregory. She hoped there would be children, but had no inkling as to when they'd come along, or how many there would be. She turned a pensive gaze to Gregory, and found him watching her. His eyes held affection, and she exhaled, knowing that whatever the road ahead held for the two of them, they would face it together.

As the meal continued, Marie chattered on a bit, expressing her excitement about the upcoming wedding. Angel found that endearing, and it enhanced her own excitement. She told Marie about the cake being made by Ruby Parker, and her nearly completed wedding gown. Lilly Benigno had been working since the third week of November to create a bridal gown for her, and she was due to have her final fitting tomorrow. The satin fabric she'd chosen was the color of rich, fresh cream, and she couldn't wait to see Gregory's face when she walked toward him at their candlelit ceremony.

When they'd had dessert and coffee, Angel stood.

Once again, the Simmons men all stood when she did.

Angel giggled. "What gentlemen. You can sit down now, I'll clear away the dishes."

Luke waved his hand. "Nonsense. You've cooked this glorious meal for us. We men will clear the table."

Gregory agreed. "Yes, my love. Now you sit."

So she did, and she and Marie watched as they cleared the dishes and took them to the sink behind the bar counter.

While they were gone, Angel leaned closer to Marie. "Your menfolk always spoil you like this?"

Marie smiled. "They treat me like a china doll, but that's all Randall's doing, I suppose."

She remembered Gregory's mention of that name. "You mean, Gregory's grandfather?"

With a nod, Marie continued. "He's of a mind that women are like rare collectibles, to be kept on a shelf. He raised Nigel that way, and Nigel's passed it on. I'm allowed to take care of them, and do housework, but not much else."

"That certainly does explain a lot about Gregory." She turned over Marie's words in her mind, thinking of how rigid Gregory had been in his attitudes about women. Perhaps he'd just been doing as the men who raised him had instructed; trying to protect her by keeping her on the proverbial shelf.

"He told me you were concerned that we wouldn't accept you, because of your race."

Angel asked, "Do Nigel and Luke know?"

Marie shook her head. "Heavens, no. There was no need to tell them."

Angel inhaled, steeling herself for whatever might come next.

"I know you must have had to bear the evil looks and the shunning of bigots, of those who think less of you simply because of your skin color. Some may even have said hateful things to you since you and my son started courting."

She'd heard a few nasty comments, but just as she'd done as a child, she'd made the choice to ignore them. Not wanting to bring up those things now, she gave her full attention to what Marie was saying.

"We're not of that ilk, dear. All Nigel and I want is for our sons to find wives who will love them, and bear them strong children. We wouldn't disapprove of you unless we thought you didn't really love him."

She exhaled. "I truly do love him, Mrs. Simmons. With all my heart."

"I know. That's why we're so happy he found you." She gave her shoulder a gentle squeeze.

That small gesture of affection brought up memories of Aunt Myrna, and the years of loving counsel she'd given her. Angel let a smile spread across her face at the impetus of the memory.

Over the sounds of the men washing the dishes in the basin, Marie said, "I can tell you'll be a wonderful addition to the Simmons family."

She embraced Marie again. "I believe that as well."

Kianna Alexander

Chapter 17

The Taylor Hotel's lobby had been transformed once again, this time for the marriage ceremony of Gregory and Angel. The space looked truly beautiful, with the lit candles set up around the room chasing away the early evening shadows. A beautifully decorated Christmas tree, festooned in shades of red and gold, occupied one corner of the lobby. The many chairs that had been set up in rows faced the ribbon draped bower, and many of the town's citizens were present to witness the nuptials.

Beneath the bower, Gregory stood in his new black suit and cream colored tie. He held the black Stetson in one hand, tapping it against his thigh. Buck and Noah, who he'd asked to stand up with him, were waiting nearby. All eyes were directed toward the stairs, waiting for the bride's descent. No one in the room was more anxious to see her than Gregory.

The violin trio began to play a slow, lilting tune. On cue, the women who'd been chosen to stand up with Angel made their way down the stairs. First came Lilly Benigno, then Prissy Parker. Last was Lupe, who would serve as maid of honor. Each woman wore a pink gown, and carried a small bunch of lilies. The three made their way down the aisle, taking their place by the bower.

The tune changed, and Angel appeared at the top of the stairs.

The moment he saw her, Gregory's breath escaped him on a sigh. His hat slipped unnoticed from his hand. Somehow, tonight, she managed to look even more beautiful than she did every other day. Her eyes held his as she made her way slowly down the stairs, arm in arm with Bernard Ridgeway. Her hair was swept up and away from her face, and held back with a row of gleaming pearls. The gown, a shoulder baring design that hugged her torso and flared into a full, lace edged skirt, was expertly fitted to accentuate her figure. Gregory took in the sight of her slowly, then let his gaze meet her eyes again. He knew his thoughts should be purer at a moment like this, but he found himself consumed by thoughts of stripping the elaborate gown from her and revealing her soft flesh to his touch.

After what seemed like a lifetime, she finally reached him.

Reverend Derrick Chase asked, "Who gives this woman to be married to this man?"

Bernard answered with a smile. "I do." And he slipped Angel's hand into Gregory's, and took his seat.

Reverend Chase proceeded with the ceremony. Gregory held both of Angel's hands in his own, looking into her eyes as he said the words. Never before had he been so sincere in any promise as when he vowed to love and cherish her, until death.

When the pronouncement was made, he drew her into his arms and kissed her lips fully. He heard the hoots of his friends and the cheers going up in the room, but he ignored them and dragged the kiss out as long as propriety would allow. When they separated, she looked up at him with sparkling, smiling eyes.

"I love you, Gregory."

He kissed her brow. "Not nearly as much as I love you, Angel May."

He felt a tap on his shoulder, and turned to see a grinning Buck, holding out his hat.

"You dropped this, pal." He winked.

"Hold on to it for me." Gregory chuckled, and linked arms with his new wife. Amid the cheers of the folks present, they strolled down the aisle toward the open doors of the dining room.

The cake Ruby had prepared was a four tiered masterpiece in sugar, and Gregory thoroughly enjoyed feeding a small piece of it to Angel. A wicked gleam sparked in her eyes as she suckled a bit of butter cream from his fingertips, making his desire rise to the point of near bursting.

After they enjoyed a bit of cake and punch, he twirled Angel around the floor for their first dance.

As they circled the room a fourth time, he leaned close to her ear and asked, "How much longer do we have to stay?"

She kissed his jaw. "We can go now if you desire, husband."

"You have no idea just how much I desire."

So Gregory spoke briefly with his parents, to let them know that he was about to whisk his bride away. When he left his smiling father and happy, but damp-eyed mother, he went to seek out Buck, who handed him a rolled piece of paper, tied with silk ribbon. Gregory tucked the paper into the inner pocket of his jacket, thanking Buck for its safekeeping. He then spirited Angel out of the dining room, leading her upstairs while the party continued on without them.

They were about halfway up the stairs when a male voice called after them. "Wait!"

Gregory groaned, but stopped climbing, and turned toward the voice with his arm still wrapped around his wife's waist. Her gaze followed his.

There, standing in near the hotel door, stood Nathan Greer.

"What do you want, Greer?" Gregory let his eyes sweep over the former mayoral candidate, and he could see the changes in his appearance right away.

Gone were the fancy clothes; Greer wore a plain, rather drab brown suit. Also gone was the bluster and puffery Greer had displayed just a few weeks ago. Greer's expression held no more pretense or haughtiness. His eyes held only sadness, defeat, and regret.

Greer, removing his bowler hat and holding it in front of him, offered a crooked half-smile. "You two look very fine today, Deputy. Very fine, indeed."

Gregory rolled his eyes. While he did sense a change in Greer, he couldn't muster a lot of interest in idle conversation with him. "Mr. Greer, if you have something to say, say it."

Greer wrung his hands. "I just wanted to apologize again. You know, for what Jim and Billy did you and Mrs. Corcoran, Angel-- I mean, Mrs. Simmons. I swear, I didn't send them. I didn't know anything about it."

Gregory swung his eyes to Angel.

She appeared to be considering his words, but didn't speak.

Greer spoke again. "I'm leaving town. After what happened, Perry threw me out. All over town, folks blame me for what happened. There's nothing here for me now."

Gregory held his bride a bit tighter to his side. "Good luck, Mr. Greer." He let his gaze communicate that he wouldn't be held up from celebrating his marriage any longer.

Greer seemed to take the hint. He began backing toward the door. "Congratulations to both of you. I really mean it."

As Gregory watched, Greer placed the bowler back atop his head, and slipped out of the hotel.

Her eyes conveying confusion, she looked up at him. "Do you think he's telling the truth? That those two goons acted on their own?"

He shrugged. "There's no telling. But right now, all I want to do is get you upstairs, and get this union properly consummated."

A smile spread across her lovely face. Grasping his hand, she tugged it gently, and they started up the stairs again.

Outside the door to his suite, he unlocked the door, then scooped her up into his arms in a rustle of silk. Tapping the door open with his foot, he carried his bride over the threshold, placed her gently on the bed, then shut and locked the door behind them.

***

Sitting atop the bed, Angel wanted nothing more than to be released from the layers of fabric encasing her body. Every cell within her cried out for her husband's touch, and she wondered if it would be too improper if she simply pounced on him.

He looked so handsome, standing there in his fine suit, watching her. From the torrid glances he'd been giving her all day, she imagined he was just as ready for lovemaking as she was. Yet, now that they were finally in the privacy of his room, she sensed some hesitation.

"Honey, Is something troubling you?" She watched him take off his hat, then carefully remove his dark jacket.

"I have a gift for you."

She smiled. "How sweet. Having you as my husband is gift enough, though."

He reached into the inner pocket of the jacket, which he'd slung over his arm, and extracted a rolled, ribbon tied piece of paper. Confusion knit her brow as he tossed the jacket aside, then walked across the room to the bed.

He offered the paper to her. "Here, my love."

She took it, carefully untied the ribbon, When she unrolled the paper, it took her a moment to figure out what she was looking at. Once she did, her hand flew to her cheek in surprise. Tears filling her eyes, she said, "A house? You've bought us a house?"

He nodded. "I've paid most of it off with my savings. Rod Emerson says his crew will begin construction just after the new year, and it should be ready by spring."

Tears spilled onto her cheeks, and she clutched the paper to her chest. "Oh, Gregory. Thank you. Thank you so much for this."

With a slow, gentle hand, he caressed her face. "You deserve it, my love. We'll move into it, and fill it with babies as soon as it suits you."

She wiped the moisture from her eyes with the back of her

hand. "I can tell you now, it won't suit me until we've made love in every room."

His eyes darkened with desire. "I can agree to that."

She met his gaze and set the blueprint aside, placing it on the side table near the bed lest it be crushed and destroyed.

He pulled her close, enfolding her in his arms, and placed his lips to hers. The kiss was as sweet as a summer ripened peach, and more filled with passion than any they'd ever shared before. She wrapped her arms around his neck and gave herself over to him, and to the sensations of his tongue searching the cavern of her mouth.

His hands behind her began touring her back, the heat of his touch seeming to penetrate the fabric of her dress and the chemise beneath it. He pulled his lips away from hers and began to place humid kisses along her cheek, her chin, the hollow of her neck, and her collarbone.

She let him have his way as long as she could stand it. Then she gently pushed him away so she could get up.

He fell back, his eyes on her.

Standing next to the bed, she gestured for him to undo her dress. Once he'd opened the hooks and eyes for her, she stepped out of the gown and draped it over the chair with his jacket. Now she wore only the lacy white chemise she'd chosen with his pleasure in mind. She's forgone any other undergarments.

He gasped when the thin garment came into view. "My God, you're lovely."

She did a slow turn to let him experience the full effect of the garment, knowing it was mostly sheer. Facing him again, she knelt to remove his shoes and socks. "Stand up, husband."

He did as she asked, and she could see his manhood straining against the fabric of his trousers. A smile lifted the corners of her mouth as she undid the buttons of his crisp shirt and removed it, tossing it away. Next she stripped him of his trousers, freeing his hardness to her touch. When her hands closed around him, she heard him groan. She stroked him, reveling in the way he sighed for her. She continued her ministrations until his hand closed over hers, staying her.

He sighed her name. "Angel."

"Don't worry, husband. I will make it all better." She placed her hands on his chest, and gently pressed until he lay across the bed on his back.

She crawled atop him, centering her core over his erect need. She recalled having tried to make love with him this way before, only to have him stop her. Now, there was no protest from him. He clasped his big hands on her waist in welcome. She lowered herself onto his hardness, and a low moan escaped her as he filled her fully. She remained still for a moment, savoring the feel of having him inside of her. Then she began to move, circling her hips and letting her body rise and fall with the building sensation.

The fire of ecstasy started low in her belly, the glow of it radiating from her center out to the tips of her fingers and toes. Every cell in her body felt alive, and in tune with him. He raised his torso from the bed, moved his hands around to cup her breasts. She leaned low for him and he drew her nipples into his mouth; first one, then the other. He then sat up, grasped her calves to pull her legs around his waist. She found that she enjoyed this position, as it still allowed her control, but put them face to face. She kissed his lips, her hips still rotating. As he wrapped his arms around her, she could feel her completion rising. The blooming joy made her pick up her pace, riding him in earnest.

His heavy breaths turned to short, throaty groans and he began to move with her, rocking his hips toward hers in time. Their bodies pressed together so closely, she felt as if they were truly one. Moments later, the sensations exploded, and she shouted his name on the wings of joy.

He kept moving inside her, even as she trembled in orgasmic bliss. Then he came with a roar of his own, his muscular arms tightening around her upper body.

She rested her head on his sweat damp shoulder, feeling the tears spring to her eyes. At this moment, intertwined with the man she loved more than anything, life had reached the apex of happiness. The new year would bring them so much- new careers, a new home, and possibly a new life in the form of a child. Whatever was ahead for them, she knew that she would always treasure this night, and this moment of pure joy in his arms.

Later, she lay in his arms after a third session of lovemaking, her body sore but sated.

"Darling?"

Only his soft snores answered her question.

A smile on her face, she snuggled in against her husband's warm body, and closed her eyes.

There would be plenty of time to talk to him later. After all, their entire life together lay ahead of them.

Kianna Alexander

Epilogue

Thaddeus Stern brushed his hand over the shoulder of his freshly pressed white shirt, then straightened. The new year was just two days old, and already it was off to a wonderful start.

He stood in the lobby of the Taylor hotel, where the chairs had been set up once again for today's event. From his spot near the windows facing Founder's Avenue, he had a good view of it all. Next to him stood his boss man, Gregory Simmons, along with his smiling wife Angel May Simmons. Husband and wife wore similar attire: denims, white shirts, and brown leather vests. Thad couldn't help noticing the gleam of happiness in Gregory's eyes, and the way he clutched his wife's hand. Seeing them made him think of his own future. He knew Gregory was excited to be promoted today, but it looked as if his truest joy came from the love of his wife.

He quickly scanned the crowd, knowing he would see Janice there. The schoolmarm loved to stay well informed on the political scene, and would not miss an event like this. Since school was still closed for the winter break, there would be no duties to keep her away.

He finally spotted her near the back, sitting in a chair close to the hotel's double doors. His pulse quickened, as it always did when he sensed her nearness. She'd done her hair up in the same conservative high bun she wore in it most of the time. Her lithe body was encased in a sunny yellow shirtwaist and simple black skirt, and he could see the gleam on the pair of pearl bobs in her ears. She didn't seem to notice his scrutiny; the slight furrow of her brow told him she was concentrating on what was being said up front. He knew he should do the same, but he watched her for a few minutes more, taking in her soft, unadorned beauty.

He turned away from her reluctantly, focusing his attention on the goings-on. Before the many citizens of town who'd come to witness the event, Bernard Ridgeway passed his official mayor's gavel to Noah Rogers.

The air was abuzz with the excitement of the occasion. Thad felt it as well, and looked forward to taking the new position he'd be awarded today. Still, he did his best to keep his face impassive. He watched the new mayor step behind the podium to make a speech.

Noah, dressed in a fine black suit with a crisp white shirt beneath, cleared his throat. "People of Ridgeway, it is my honor to become your mayor today. I'd like to give my thanks to all who contributed in any way to my campaign, including casting a ballot in my favor. I want my tenure as mayor to be remembered as a time of positive change in our town, and so I plan to set in motion all the things I've promised as soon as possible."

A smattering of applause filled the hotel's lobby, the citizens expressing their approval.

Noah continued. "I will work with the town council, as well as the citizens of this great town, to do what is best for us all. My first acts as mayor today will be to appoint our new sheriff, and deputy sheriff. Gregory, Thad, please come up."

He gestured for Greg and his missus to go first, then followed them to the podium. He stood at attention while Noah made the appointments.

Noah pinned the gold sheriff's star to the right side of Gregory's vest. "Gregory Simmons, I hereby appoint you sheriff of Ridgeway."

Thad watched the light of pride dancing in Mrs. Simmon's eyes as the pinning was done.

Now Noah moved toward him, with the silver deputy's star in his hand. "Thaddeus Stern, I hereby appoint you deputy sheriff of Ridgeway."

The pin slid through the leather of his vest, and clicked

into place. He reached out to shake Noah's hand. "Thank you sir."

Noah moved back to the podium. "Folks, we have a grand surprise. Our new sheriff has another announcement to make."

A collective gasp rose in the room, as well as a lot of speculative chatter.

Thad only smiled, well aware of what was coming.

Noah handed a silver shield to Gregory, who faced the assembled crowd.

Gregory's voice filled the space. "My first edict as sheriff is that we will now be actively seeking female officers for our police force. If I'm honest, I must say I was inspired by my wife." He placed a chaste kiss on her cheek.

There were a few male grumbles from the crowd.

Gregory continued. "From now on, any woman who feels she has the courage and goodwill for her neighbors to pursue a career in law enforcement is welcome to apply for a position. I'll expect to see many of you stopping by the office in the coming weeks."

But the women in the room drowned them out as they jumped to their feet, cheering and clapping. Janice was among them, and Thad couldn't help smiling as he watched her displaying her happiness. The bright smile she wore, and the merriment dancing in her brown eyes, easily made her the most beautiful creature in the room.

Noah banged his gavel, tempering the celebration. "I have one further announcement to make. I've spoken with Rod Emerson, and I am pleased to announce that in the spring, we will break ground on a new concert hall and theater here in Ridgeway: the Myrna Lane Corcoran Performance Hall."

Another round of cheers went up. Thad looked to the newly minted Mrs. Simmons, and saw the tears standing in her eyes. He knew she must be very proud to have her aunt honored that way.

Kianna Alexander

When the day's festivities began to wind down, Thad wove his way through the groups of townsfolk still congregating in the room. Janice was speaking with the librarian Ms. Parker, so he stood back a few steps to let them finish their conversation. When Prissy drifted away, he inched closer to Janice.

"Hello, Miss Smart." He clasped her hand, raised it to his lips for a gentlemanly kiss.

She blushed. "Hello, Deputy Stern. Congratulations on your appointment."

"Thank you." His heart thumped in his chest so loudly he swore she could hear it. They'd been secretly meeting for more than three years now, but still kept up this facade of formality in public.

She offered a small smile. "You're welcome. Tell me, how will you celebrate this occasion?"

He looked at her, and sensed a bit of teasing in her words. He leaned down near her ear, so that only she could hear. "Why, I can't think of a better way to celebrate than to steal away with you."

"Why, Deputy. It's just fortunate for you that Adam has gone back east to visit his godmother."

He knew she spoke of her nephew, whom she'd been raising since he was a tot. The boy was about ten, and as charming as could be, but Thad had to admit he was glad to get Janice to himself. "Then what are we waiting for?"

The blush deepened, but she said nothing. Instead, she clasped his hand.

He let her lead him through the open doors of the hotel, and out onto the walk.

Kianna Alexander

AUTHOR'S NOTE

I hope you enjoyed Electing to Love. Writing Gregory and Angel's story was a long and research intensive process; for a while there I had to "move" to Ridgeway, or at least I felt like it! Still, it felt good to expand the story beyond the word counts of the first three books, and give my readers the longer book they've been asking for. I tried to hit a sweet spot, giving you just enough about the character's developing relationship to help you understand their journey without overwhelming you, and just enough historical information to enlighten you without boring you. Hopefully I've achieved that goal, and you'll stick around for the next trip to Ridgeway!

I'm sure you've guessed it by now, but the next book will be Thaddeus and Janice's story. Look for <u>Lessons of the Heart</u>, The Roses of Ridgeway Book 5, either in late 2015 or early 2016. The best way to keep up with my release schedule, what I'm doing and where I'm going is to subscribe to my mailing list. Simply visit my homepage (<u>www.AuthorKiannaAlexander.com</u>) to sign up.

I love hearing from readers, so feel free to drop by my website and leave me a message via the Contact page. You can also send me a message on social media, my Facebook and Twitter information is listed below. Thank you so very much for your support.

All the Best,
-Kianna

Facebook.com/KiannaWrites
Twitter.com/KiannaWrites

Kianna Alexander

Kianna Alexander

Other Titles by Kianna Alexander

The Roses of Ridgeway (Western Historical Romance)

Kissing the Captain

The Preacher's Paramour

Loving the Lawman

Roses of Ridgeway, Volume 1 (Contains all 3 books)

Graham's Goddesses(Sensual Historical Romance)

Freedom's Embrace

Love's Lasso

Deputy's Desire

Phoenix Files (Sensual Contemporary Paranormal Romance)

Darkness Rising

Embrace the Night

Midnight's Serenade

The Phoenix Files Trilogy (Contains all 3 books)

Climax Creek Series (Erotic Contemporary Romance)

Seducing Sheri

Vying for Vivian

Adoring Ava

Persuading Patrice

Kianna Alexander

Kianna Alexander

About the Author

Kianna Alexander loves to regale readers with romantic tales that touch the heart. Kianna wears many hats: wife to her childhood sweetheart, mother to two very precocious youngsters, sister, adviser, friend, and purveyor of all things awesome. She lives in the mid-Atlantic US with her family. When not writing, she enjoys reading, listening to music, goofing off on social media, and playing hidden object games.

For more, visit the author's website:

www.AuthorKiannaAlexander.com

Find her on social media by searching "KiannaWrites" on Facebook, Twitter, and Pinterest

Kianna Alexander

Kianna Alexander

18816739R00123

Made in the USA
Middletown, DE
23 March 2015